In the Presence of Angels

Andrea Fitzpatrick

Contents

Chapter One: A second Chance 1

Chapter Two: Stranger in the Crowd 19

Chapter Three: The Angel Pin 37

Chapter Four: A New Soul 55

Chapter Five: In the Presence of Angels 73

Chapter Six: The Persistent Mr Black 90

Chapter Seven: Charlie's Golden Rules 108

Chapter Eight: Gift of a Heart 126

Chapter Nine: Angel on the Wing 144

Chapter Ten: Home Once More 161

Chapter Eleven: Follow Your Heart 177

Chapter One:
A second Chance

On a wet and blustery late autumn evening, on the Northbound carriageway of the M23 motorway south of London, there is a scene of carnage, where several fatalities and serious injuries occurred. The sound of people screaming and children crying fills the air. People are running toward the scene of the accident to see if they can offer help to the people inside. In one of the cars, a professional young lady by the name of Jana Heart is experiencing what seems to be an immediate stopping of time. The sounds around her merge into one, blood is pouring down the side of her face, she is trapped inside the vehicle unable to move. Jana is unable to make sense of the noise and the feelings that she is experiencing. In her mind, she calls out to her boyfriend, who was driving the car, she is drifting in and out of consciousness. Jana thinks she can hear her boyfriend calling her.

An older gentleman stands beside the wreckage of her car, he has come to help with the devastation. 'Stay with me, stay with me, young lady, the paramedics and ambulances are on their way' he said frantically trying to keep her conscious. Jana's boyfriend Justin had been able to get out of the car unscathed, in shock he was being helped by a woman while they waited for the ambulance to arrive. An air ambulance hovers above the section of the motorway where the accident occurred. The crew of the helicopter look for a safe place to land, they can see the police, ambulances and fire engines on the ground racing towards the scene. Traffic had come to a standstill, and people were getting out of their cars to see what was happening. The police were arriving and asking people to get back into their vehicles, while they cordoned off the area putting up tents over the cars, giving those inside the crashed vehicles protection and dignity from prying eyes and to save any destruction of evidence. It was not long before news reports began filtering through on the car radios.

There was suspicion amongst the witnesses that the accident was no coincidence and that it had been a deliberate attempt by two men to run another car off the motorway, which resulted in a pileup of multiple vehicles which caused several deaths and many injuries, some that would be life-changing. The newscaster asked for those who had dashcams to check them and see if they could provide evidence of what had happened and to contact their local police station.

#

Three years later, on a hot day in July; Jana could hear and feel the breeze as it blew through the palm tree she was sitting under, away from the searing heat of the day. Feeling the sun had burned her skin when she had been walking in it earlier that morning, Jana made sure that she put sun lotion on. The cream had little effect on her on this hot day, leading her to seek shade from under the palm tree. Jana had come to Lanzarote in the hope that she could relax and leave her demons back amongst the miserable weather in the UK. For some months, she had been feeling a sense of fear and loneliness, Jana could feel herself trembling inside, she had been feeling invisible to others around her. Jana had only arrived in Lanzarote just two days before and with the sun shining and the children laughing and playing had hoped that the break would help her to be able to relax. Jana had not been able to relax for some years, not since she had her near-death experience following the accident. After this, the feelings of despair and fear increased, and one thing Jana had learned was that these feelings could only mean one thing to her, and that was the imminent death of others. Unknown to Jana was How? When? Why? And more importantly, Who?

Jana tried to will away these feelings and prayed that she would find peace. Deep down, she knew that this would not be the case, and realised that she would have to eventually accept and face the signs that were appearing to her, no matter how much they frightened her. Jana needed to distract herself from her thoughts, and so she turned them to watching the housekeepers with their trolleys full of linen, towels and cleaning products as they moved from apartment to apartment. The veranda door was wedged open, and Jana watched as the housekeepers cleaned the apartment next to hers. Jana could smell the aroma of the polish and chemicals that were being used to clean the surfaces and floors. Jana watched the housekeeper as she polished the furniture and made up the bed at speed, she could see that the woman took pride in her work. The cleaner left the apartment and wiped her hands down over her uniform dress as if to straighten herself out. Jana turned to look at the sun and saw that it was getting higher in the sky, she checked her watch and discovered that it was almost noon, time for lunch. Jana freshened up and made her way down to the central area of the hotel complex where she is staying.

Jana had to walk by the main pool to get to the restaurant, and heard the children laughing. She looked towards the children in the pool and smiled as they tried to climb onto their inflatables of different colours and shapes only to fall straight back off them into the pool. It was a warm day, and Jana decided to sit on the veranda of the restaurant to eat her lunch; in the hope that the sound of the children laughing would make her feel less lonely. Jana picked up the menu from the centre of the table and looked briefly through it, deciding that she would have a light lunch of chicken and spinach parcels with a side salad and cold glass of lemonade. Jana continued to watch the children playing in the pool while the meal was being prepared, she watched as they splashed each other and listened to their parents laughing loudly at their children's antics in the pool. The waiter arrived with her food, as he placed the meal in front of her, the aroma of the meal heightened her sense of smell, and the presentation of the food was visually pleasing. The parcels were warm just as she liked them. Jana cut into a piece of the food; the chicken and spinach parcels were full of bacon pieces, peppers and succulent chunks of chicken. The aroma became more pungent as it filled the air around her. Jana placed a portion of the food in her mouth and appreciated the texture, the chicken was delicious, and she could taste the intense flavours of the meal dancing over her tongue.

After lunch, Jana decided to take a walk to the beach. It was a five-minute walk away from the hotel, as she walked along Jana watched the people around her shopping in the many and various types of beachfront shops that lined the promenade. She envied the couples and families, as they walked together holding hands, either with each other or with their children. Jana had been without family since her teenage years. Her thoughts drifted to the past, she remembered the car accident she had been in. An accident that Jana had survived but had been fatal for others. A small child distracted her from her thoughts as she ran past her laughing, her father chasing behind bent forward and swooped her up into his arms before running with her toward the beach. Jana reached the beach and took off her sandals; she walked toward the sea, the sand getting between her toes, she could smell the ocean as the sun continued to warm her skin. Jana decided to take a stroll in the sea, and despite the heat of the sun, the water felt cold on her feet. She walked along kicking up the water, she had been feeling quite tense but began to feel calmer as she watched the waves beat against her ankles.

Jana felt the water wash away some of the aches and pains that she had been feeling since the car accident, some years earlier. Over time she had become used to the aches and pains, and always felt relief from the sea when she walked in it. Jana began to remember the time of the accident. Still, she could not recall the accident itself. What she did remember, Jana knew would remain with her the rest of her life.

#

It had been a close call for Jana; she had been at death's door after the accident. It was on the operating table following the crash that she had experienced seeing spirit for the first time. Jana remembered going through a dark tunnel, towards a bright white light. She remembered how the darkness had surrounded her, the only light that could be seen was ahead of her. Jana did not know what was happening to her, but as the brightness got closer, it was found that it did not hurt her eyes. As Jana went through the tunnel, she could feel the pain that she experienced because of the accident fade away. The closer Jana got to the light; the pain became less intense. Jana began to feel a calmness come over her, and as she entered the brightness of the tunnel, she could see people she knew who had died many years before. The light became more significant as it engulfed her entire body. Jana found herself standing on a road; a road she had been familiar with growing up as a child, she was now facing the very house where she had lived from a very young age.

The house stood sturdy, the front garden was vibrant with colours, and there was a variety of plants and flowers. It appeared to Jana that the colours were bouncing from petal to petal off the different flowers, the colours changing and intermingling as they did so. In front of the house stood various members of her family and friends. Along with the calmness, Jana also felt love; a love that she had never felt as endearing and profound in her entire life as she did at this moment in time. As Jana looked at her family and friends, she could not believe what she was seeing. How was it possible to see them? They had all died, some when she was very young. As she continued to watch, she saw her maternal grandparents step down from the front doorstep, smiling and waving at her. Jana watched as another couple replaced them on the step; she recognised them instantly. She could hear her father speak; she was alarmed to see his lips were not moving. How is this possible? Jana thought to herself.

Jana watched as they walked down into the garden to meet her. In what seemed to be in a blink of an eye, they stood in front of her. Jana's father held her in his arms for a short while, before stepping aside to let her mother do the same. Jana could feel the tears stream down her face, her mother smiled at her and held out her arms, Jana could feel the tenderness as her mother held her close. Jana's father stepped back to her side and began speaking to her.

#

'Your life journey has not come to an end; you need to go back to help others. You have been given a special gift, and your future is to work with the angels and your spirit guides. Jana, you have been given the gift of a second chance, so that you can help others, as you have been helped in your hour of need.'

#

All too soon it was over, and Jana could feel herself being pulled back through the tunnel at high speed. At the end of the tunnel, Jana felt as if she was floating, she looked around and saw how close the ceiling was to her.

Jana looked down and realised that she could see her body lying on the operating table, and although unconscious Jana could hear people shouting around her, she could not understand what everyone was saying as everything sounded muffled. Jana screamed for them to all leave her alone, to let her go back to her family, no one responded to her cries. Jana; now in the recovery room, gradually began to regain consciousness, the more awake she became, the more uncomfortable the pain and nausea became. Jana slipped into unconsciousness again. The next time she woke, it was to find herself in a bed in a hospital ward. A fan was blowing in her face; with only a sheet on her body and dressed in the hospital gown that had been worn in the operating theatre, Jana began to shake violently. Shouting out for the fan to be turned off, and for someone to get some more blankets, she felt cold and was scared; she had never felt this cold in her life before. Jana could feel the cold as if it were in her bones. A nurse tended to her needs, 'You have a high temperature, and we need to get it back to normal, a doctor will be here to see you shortly, in the meantime let me go and get you some medications to help you with your temperature and pain,' the nurse said before she left the room to seek out the medications that were needed.

A little while later, the doctor arrived at her bedside, pulling the curtains around them for privacy. He sat down and began to explain to Jana what had happened to her. He told Jana that she had been in a multi-car pileup and that she was fortunate to be alive. He explained that she had fractured her skull and lost her left forearm and hand due to the crash, he assured her that he and his team had done everything they could to save them. The doctor went on to explain that they had removed her arm just below the elbow. Jana looked down to see the emptiness where her arm should be, she turned away from the doctor and began to cry bitterly. Why did she not notice that her arm and hand were missing? The doctor slipped out through the curtains; he called the nurse over and pointed to Jana's medication chart; he instructed the nurse to give Jana some medication to help with the shock. The nurse followed the doctor's instruction, and with a glass of water gave Jana the drug, she sat with Jana monitoring her closely, Jana was not just a patient she was a friend, they had both gone to the same university to train. Soon after and with the tablet talking effect; still sobbing Jana fell asleep.

Jana slept for a few hours until gradually, she began to wake, thoughts began racing through her mind, and she was uncertain of her future. Jana did not know what she would do and how she would be able to cope. Her career as a physiotherapist had allowed her to fulfil her need to care for others. She now felt that this was a job that will be more difficult without the full use of her arm. Colleagues and friends visited Jana at the hospital and tried to encourage her to continue with her career, the more Jana thought about it, the more difficult in her mind the job became for her. Some days later, as Jana lay in her bed, the pain became unbearable again. Jana pressed the buzzer to call the nurse and asked for pain relief; she did not like taking medications but knew that the pain would not subside without them. As the drugs took effect and Jana became drowsy, she fell into a deep sleep. Sometime later, Jana woke to the darkness outside the window. On waking, she looked around the ward at the other patients; it was then that she saw what looked like small lights bouncing around the room. Jana glanced in the direction of the other patients again, and she could see some reading and others watching television. Not one of the other patients seemed to notice the lights.

Jana blinked and blinked, thinking her eyes were playing tricks on her. She could feel her heart beating in her chest as they came closer to her, the lights began to get bigger the closer they got to Jana, and they began to form shapes that were changing rapidly. Unexpectedly, the most beautiful being she had ever seen stood in front of her, Jana no longer felt scared as she looked upon the eyes of the angel that stood before her.

#

Jana was pulled from her memories of that day as her thoughts were distracted, and she was back to the present. She could hear people screaming and shouting for help. Jana looked towards the noise, as she watched she could see people dragging a lifeless body out of the sea. Everyone around froze to the spot; no one seemed to know what to do. Jana reacted instantly and ran up the beach as fast as she could, as she did so, she forgot all her worries. There on the sand lay a young man, Jana knelt before him and searched for a pulse. She watched eagerly for his chest to rise and fall. Her worst fears were growing as the young man had stopped breathing. Jana screamed for people around her to call for an ambulance. She continued to assess the young man further, and as she did so, all her training came to the forefront of her mind. As a physiotherapist, resuscitation had been part of her mandatory training.

Jana shouted to one of the young men standing around. 'I am going to need your help' Jana was speaking as she lifted her prosthetic arm towards him, so he would see the difficulty that she would have alone. Jana feared that she would cause him further injury if she used the prosthetic arm to press on his chest.

'I don't know what to do' he said

'What's your name? Do you know him? Jana asked, pointing to the young man on the sand.

'Yes, I'm Chris, that's Callum, he's my friend. Is he going to be alright?' he replied anxiously.

Jana knew that time was critical, in situations like this and that they would have to resuscitate him immediately.

'Chris, we are going to have to act quickly, I will tell you what to do ok' Jana said

'Ok,' he said, shaking.

'You are going to have to do the compressions, place your hand on his chest this way' Jana showed him how to hold his hands as she continued to direct him.

'Right, place your hands there and push up and down into his chest to a count of thirty, at thirty, you stop, and I will give him two breaths. Before I check to see if he is breathing on his own, listen to my instructions, ok. Jana was mindful of the time, 'we have to start Chris' Jana said firmly. While she had been explaining things to Chris, Jana had checked to see if there were any foreign objects in Callum's mouth and throat.

As she tilted his head back, she could see it was clear. Jana instructed Chris to begin the compressions into Callum's chest and asked him to count aloud as he did so. Chris started to count; One, Two, Three, Four, Five. When he reached thirty, he stopped the compressions and Jana took over, she leaned over Callum and putting her prostatic hand under his chin tilted his head back to open his airways, she pinched his nostrils together and sealed her lips around his. Jana began the breaths, one, two, she counted in her head, as she breathed into his mouth she watched to see if his chest was rising. Callum continued to have difficulty, and they repeated the procedure one more time, they were both beginning to feel tired. The effort to resuscitate Callum was becoming exhausting, no one around them wanted to help, and some were even drifting away. Unexpectedly, Callum began to cough and splutter as the seawater he had inhaled while unconscious spurt out of his mouth. Jana immediately put him in the recovery position, just as she did so the ambulance arrived.

Jana explained to the paramedics what had happened with the resuscitation before slipping away unnoticed. The ambulance crew checked Callum over and put him into the back of the ambulance with Chris firmly by his side, telling them what had happened to his friend. Jana began to walk back to the hotel; she could feel her head pounding and so decided that she would take some pain relief and have a laydown. Jana hoped that this would help the pain to go away, it was a while before she fell asleep. When Jana woke it was to feel hunger pangs and realising that she had not had a meal for some time, she quickly showered, got dressed and headed for the restaurant. Jana entered the restaurant and asked for a seat by the window. She took in the atmosphere of the restaurant; she had seen a few hotel restaurants, but this one was quaint, its décor was of ivory and gold. The wallpaper looked expensive with an ivory background, and a pattern of gold leaves spread out over it. Lights were placed strategically on the walls giving the room a low, warm glow. 'Are you ready to order now miss?' the waiter asked as he stood over her, making her jump a little. Jana skimmed the menu one more time before placing her order for a light meal and a glass of white wine.

While she waited, she continued to take in the ambience of the dining room. As the waiter arrived with her meal, Jana could hear the couple sitting at the next table; the woman was excitingly asking her companion if he had seen what had happened on the beach while he was there that afternoon, the gentleman told her that he had not seen anything to her dismay. The woman went on to say to him about the young man whose life had been saved by a woman. She went on to tell him how the woman had seemed to vanish into thin air,

'Vanished I tell you' she repeated

'No one can simply vanish' replied her companion

'Well, this one did,' replied the woman as she eagerly tried to convince him of the truth of the matter. Jana smiled to herself as she listened to them argue over who was right and who was wrong. Following her meal, Jana went into the lounge to watch the entertainment provided by the hotel. As she listened to the music, her thoughts drifted off, back to the time in the hospital room where she had seen the angel for the first time.

Jana felt apprehensive upon recalling the moment. She had looked around at the other patients, but no one else could see the angel. She remembered that the angel had a glow around its body and how it had appeared to be floating. The beauty of the angel was unworldly, Jana heard the angel talking to her, again there had been no movement of the lips. Jana recalled how she had listened to her father, speaking to her without moving his lips. Jana remembered the words the angel had spoken to her as if the angel were right there in front of her repeating them. 'I have been sent to help you' the angel said

'Who sent you?' Jana asked

'It was you,' the angel replied 'in your darkest hour you called out and asked for help' replied the angel. Unexpectedly Jana was back in the car; her arm trapped; she remembers crying out, 'Help me someone, please help me' before she went unconscious.

Jana's thoughts were disturbed once more as she heard someone talk to her, 'Is there anyone sitting here?' It was the woman from the dining room, as she asked, she was sitting herself down next to Jana at her table. Jana wanted to tell her that she wanted to be on her own but thought better of it, she was not rude by nature and instead introduced herself to the woman. 'Please take a seat. I'm Jana'

'Nice to meet you, I'm, Rachel' replied the woman, as she sat back and listened to the singer. The waiter came over to the table, and Jana ordered a bottle of wine and two glasses to share with Rachel. As the music played, the two women got chatting, getting to know each other better. 'What happened to your arm?' Rachel asked, as she observed Jana's arm. Jana lowered her head and told her about the accident and how she had lost her arm because of the crash. 'That is terrible, do you remember it?' Rachel asked.

'To be honest, I remember some of it, but I don't know if I want to remember' said Jana.

The subject was then dropped unanimously and quietly by both women as they turned to watch the singer and listen to music. They continued to chat intermittently, getting to know more about each other and each other's lives, the subject of the accident did not resurface in the conversation. The waiter arrived with another bottle of wine, as they drank the wine; they became more and more relaxed. Jana found herself to be enjoying the night and Rachels company as they sang to the tunes and giggled randomly. Rachel's husband came over to join them, 'Jana this is my husband.   Stuart, this is Jana' Rachel said as she introduced them to each other,

'Hi Jana, nice to meet you' Stuart said as he reached over to shake Jana's hand.

Time went by quickly; it was past midnight before they retired to bed. Jana fell asleep with a smile on her face as she reflected on the evening. Deep in sleep, she was again plunged into a dream; The streetlights were glowing 'Where am I?' Jana looked around and not recognising where she was, she became frightened. Jana could hear car engines and people talking in a muffled voice, she looked at them but found it impossible to make out their faces or what they looked like, who they were or where she was. As the dream continued, Jana began to walk the street finding herself getting closer to the figures, 'Why am I walking towards them?' She thought to herself. Jana could make out by their voices and stance that they were males. As Jana got closer to the men; she could see that a car had pulled up next to them. Jana watched as another man got out of the vehicle, the man looked directly at her. The dream was so vivid it felt like she was there, it felt like she was awake. Jana gasped realising the man had no face; Jana could not move and felt rooted to the spot. She watched as the two men bundled the third man into the car, she tried to shout at them to leave him alone. No sound came from her mouth, Jana could hear herself speaking words, but there was no sound.

Waking abruptly, she found that she was covered in sweat, and her heart was beating loudly in her chest. Jana had been experiencing these reoccurring nightmares most nights since the accident. Each night when she had the dream, it would reveal more detail to her. Jana always felt disturbed by the visions, and when she woke, she did not understand why she was having the dreams. Jana looked at the clock on the bedside table; it showed that it was five o'clock in the morning; shaking she got dressed and went to the reception. There was no one around except for night security; she decided to go for a walk on the beach, the sea was clear, the rising sun's rays bounced around as it reflected on the water. Jana began to feel calmer; the sea had always had that effect on her, she had loved the sea ever since she was a little girl, she had fond memories of day trips to the beach with her grandparents. Jana remembered how they would look for crabs under the rocks and how on a hot day they would sit on the sand having a picnic. She had lost her grandparents in her teenage years, and since then, whenever she felt sad or lonely, she would head for the beach, this had always made her feel closer to them. Jana looked down at her watch, it was fast approaching nine o'clock, and the shops were beginning to open.

Jana headed back to have some breakfast; she had booked herself on an excursion to one of the local markets and needed to be sure she was ready to leave on time. As she arrived back at the reception, she spotted Rachel and Stuart and waved at them. Passing them, Jana saw that they were in a deep conversation with another couple. She needed to rush to catch the coach to the market, there had been a disruption in the kitchens of the hotel restaurant, and her meal had not come. Jana reached the bus stop a little short of breath; she had been running to make sure she made it in time. Only just making it as the coach pulled up to the bus stop at the same time as her. While on the coach, Jana took in the scenery, she watched as the coach passed by the dry arid land that had some green shrubbery and trees scattered about. While the coach made its journey to the market, she began drifting off again back to the past. Jana could never understand why she could remember being in the accident, but could not remember what had happened, before the crash. Jana had been a happy go lucky young woman with hopes and dreams of marriage and a family; the accident had put a stop to all that. *"Who would want to be with me now?" Jana thought.*

#

Thinking about her past, she recalled her ex-boyfriend Justin; she had been with him for four years before the accident. Jana had met him when she was out on her Christmas outing with her colleagues, they had gone into the city on a pub crawl and ended up in a nightclub. It was here Jana met Justin. Justin had been working behind the bar of the nightclub, and she thought he was a handsome man. Amongst the loud noise of the music playing, Jana had been chatting away to her colleagues; when she looked up, it was to see Justin staring at her from behind the bar as he served people their drinks. Jana smiled, and Justin smiled back in response. She saw Justin once more that night as he arrived at her table to collect empty glasses. 'Hi, my name is Justin' he said as he leaned close to her ear to introduce himself, amongst the noise of the club. Justin handed Jana a piece of paper with his phone number on and told her to ring him so they could arrange a time to go out. Justin watched as Jana put the note into her bag before he went back to work. Jana had been unsure what to make of him and his directness.

They saw a lot of each other over the coming months, and their relationship blossomed and had been a healthy one, or so Jana had thought. They enjoyed spending time together, but they both made sure that they kept a healthy social life and would often meet up with friends to go out for a meal and a drink. Justin would spend time with his friends, usually going abroad with the boys, sometimes for two weeks at a time. Justin always made sure that he contacted her while away until the accident that is, it was then that he changed towards her. Justin had been the one driving the day of the accident, that much Jana could remember. He had only visited her once since the crash, and when he did, she saw him acting strangely. Justin kept repeating the words 'I'm sorry, I'm sorry,' and he kept looking at the ward doorway throughout the visit. Jana took this to be Justin feeling guilty about the accident and was eager to get away from her. 'It was an accident; you have nothing to be sorry about' Jana tried to reassure him. Justin held Jana's hand, looking into her eyes said, 'I love you with all my heart, I promise we will get through this together. Jana, I will always be here for you.' Justin lent over to kiss Jana as he was leaving, he smiled and waved from the doorway. Jana never saw him again. Neither of them had ended the relationship, but Jana knew it was over. She was alone now, she had no family left, Jana was an only child, so there were no siblings, and she had lost all contact with her paternal relatives after her grandparents died. Jana had seen little of her maternal family and only remembers seeing them once when she was a small child.

#

The screeching of the brakes as the coach pulled up at the market, brought Jana back to the present moment. Her thoughts again pushed to the back of her mind. As she got off the air-conditioned coach to the heat of the day, she felt in need of some refreshments. Spotting an ice cream cart which had her favourite Italian pistachio ice cream on it, she delighted in purchasing one and enjoyed it as she strolled around the stalls. It was busy at the market; Jana could see crowds of people both locals and holidaymakers bustling through, checking out the stalls. Jana wandered through the stalls looking at the offerings and found herself purchasing a silk scarf and some new sandals from a local lady that was selling goods imported from Morocco in Africa. Jana then went to look for an area where she could sit and enjoy an ice-cold drink in the shade. Sitting there, Jana could see a man watching her from across the way. She had noticed him a couple of times walking around the market but thought nothing of it until now. Why was he watching her? The man approached and sat beside her. He did not speak, just occasionally looked at her. Jana began to feel uncomfortable; she did not have a good feeling about this man.

She hurried off back to the coach; it was an hour before the coach was due to leave the market, but that didn't matter, she felt safer on the coach; the stranger had startled her. Nervously Jana kept looking out for the strange man, his actions had made her feel very vulnerable. Jana was scared; no man had ever made her feel this way before. She had always been an active and independent woman and had known what she had wanted out of life since being a small child. Jana had never had to rely on anyone, not since the passing of her parents and grandparents. Jana knew she had changed since the accident and longed for the old stronger Jana she once knew to return. Jana could not allow herself to drift back into the past this time. She had to remain aware of who was around her. Jana could see the coach driver outside smoking a cigarette; this made her feel a little more relaxed but still not safe enough. The passengers were boarding the coach now for the return trip back.

Jana sat at the front of the coach; she felt too alarmed to sit at the back on her own. Jana was afraid the strange man would get on the bus when she was alone. An elderly gentleman sat down beside her and asked, 'Do you mind if I sit here?'

'No' replied Jana, she felt safer now that someone was sitting next to her. Soon the coach was full, and they were on their way. Jana felt a sigh of relief come over her; she must have sighed out loud as the elderly gentleman asked her 'Are you alright?' he observed her for a moment before saying 'don't worry, everything will be alright.' Jana smiled in response; the elderly gentleman changed the subject and introduced himself.

'I'm George' he said. Jana smiled and introduced herself to him, and they enjoyed the rest of the journey, chatting, mostly about his wife. 'My wife, Emily, passed away two years ago. I miss her terribly,' he said. George went on to say how he had longed to be with her again. 'she was my rock, my saviour, she supported me through our marriage' he continued as he fondly remembered his wife. 'There was only the two of us; we were not fortunate to have children of our own' explained George as the chat continued,

'I am sorry about that' Jana replied as she felt his pain,

'It's not all sad,' he said as he took on Jana's expression to be pitiful.

George continued with the conversation and went on to say, 'My brother had a little girl, she is like our very own, the three of us did everything together.' George smiled as he remembered the past. His expression then changed to one of sorrow as he said, 'I never got to say goodbye to my niece.'

'I'm sure you will get to see her again' Jana said as she tried to reassure him. George smiled in response; his eyes, however, continued to show his sorrow. Jana turned as she heard some giggling coming from the seats around her, as Jana turned to look, she saw people staring at her, they would smile at her then turn away, unable to keep eye contact with her. Jana was puzzled as to why they were giggling at her and could not see a reason for their laughter. Jana turned back to George; she had noticed that throughout the conversation, he had intermittently looked down at her arm. George never asked, nor made any judgment, he just listened.

The journey came to an end, and as they both left the coach, Jana could see that George had a limp, she had not noticed this when he got onto the coach. She looked at his legs first, then back to his face. George smiled then knocked on his leg with his knuckles. Jana heard tapping on wood; she looked back at George, who merely winked as he looked at her arm and smiled a smile of understanding. George waved, and then he disappeared into the crowd. As Jana walked the short distance to her apartment, she could see that there were some ambulance and police. Jana attempted to go to her apartment, but the police prevented her from doing so. They had it cordoned off, she made her way to the reception area where she met Rachel and Stuart, and true to her nature Rachel excitedly informed her of the excitement at the hotel and why the authorities were there. 'There's been a death' Rachel said.

'A death, what happened?' Jana said

They all stopped chatting as they watched the police dashing back and forth.

Chapter Two:
Stranger in the Crowd

Jana could not make out whether Rachel was excited or nervous as she began to tell her what had happened.

'Some old gent went in his sleep, we think.'

'Where did you get all this information from?' asked Jana.

'His niece, she's in there,' she whispered as she pointed to the hotel managers office. As she did so, a middle-aged woman came out of the door; it had been evident that she had been crying and was upset. The manager was escorting the woman out of his office; he was speaking in broken English; it was apparent that the woman was struggling to understand him. Jana approached them with Rachel close behind her and asked if she could help, the woman turned to Jana smiled and thanked her. Between them, they were able to understand that the manager had spoken to the police and that they had arranged for an interpreter to come and talk to her. As they were both unable to get into their apartments, Jana suggested that they go to Rachels apartment. Rachel had gone back to Stuart by this time, Jana approached them both and asked if they could use their apartment until the police had dealt with the incident and allowed them back into their own.

'Of course, you can' Stuart said, without hesitation.

Jana informed the manager of the apartment number and asked if he would send the interpreter there. The manager nodded in response.

In the apartment, the middle-aged woman introduced herself, 'My name is Louise Carter, thank you for helping me, it's been such an unexpected nightmare,' she said as she looked around at them all.

'I'm Jana, and this is Rachel Camberley and her husband Stuart,' Jana said as she introduced everyone to Louise, 'Is there anybody we can contact on your behalf?' Jana asked.

'No thank you, I have already called my husband, he is going to get the earliest flight out he can in the morning.' Rachel handed Louise and Jana a cup of tea, Stuart made his excuse;

'I am so sorry for your loss, Louise; I will go and make sure the manager sends the interpreter to the right apartment' he said as he left. Louise began telling Jana and Rachel what had happened. 'I needed to go to the shop, we had run out of milk you see' she said as she began her story, 'my uncle and aunt have owned the apartment for years, I have been coming on holidays with them all my life. They were like parents to me; we are very close. Louise said as she started crying.

Rachel reached for the box of hankies that were on the coffee table and offered them to Louise. Wiping her eyes, Louise pulled herself together and continued with her story; she had gone to the shops at nine-thirty in the morning, her uncle had decided that he would go back to bed as he was feeling tired. 'This was something he would often do,' Louise continued telling them what had happened. 'I was at the shops for an hour, when I returned, I checked on my uncle and found him to be sleeping soundly, or so I thought. I should have gone into the room to check on him then' upset, Louise began to cry again, she was overwhelmed with guilt for not going into the bedroom and checking on him. Jana tried to reassure Louise, 'You could not have known what was about to happen.'

'Where is your aunt? Is she alright?' Rachel interrupted the conversation with the question.

'Oh, my aunt died some years ago' Louise replied. 'If she had been here, he would not have died alone.' She began to cry again.

'Your uncle did not want you there when he died' Jana reassured Louise. Jana knew that Louise's uncle did not want her there when he died, *"How do I know that?"* Jana thought to herself. It was like the thought had entered her mind, and she knew she had to say it. 'What were your auntie and uncle like?' Rachel interrupted again. Louise was unable to answer as there was a knock on the door. Rachel answered the door to find the manager, a policeman and another man standing there.

'Hello, my name is Carlos, this is officer Ramos who is representing the Policia Local.' 'I have been asked to interpret for the authorities' he explained to Rachel as he reached out to shake her hand. Rachel held the door open for both the interpreter and police officer to enter the apartment as the manager returned to his office. 'This is the lady you are looking for' Rachel informed Carlos as she directed him to Louise. 'Louise this is Carlos, he is the interpreter.' Carlos held out his hand to shake Louise's hand. 'Only if you agree for me to interpret for you.' Carlos said.

'yes please, I don't know what is going on, and I don't know what to do next' Louise replied. Louise introduced Jana and Rachel before they started the questioning. Carlos explained what would happen before proceeding. 'As the death is unexpected, the police would like to ask you some questions,' he said. Carlos looked towards Jana and Rachel and asked Louise, 'Would you like to discuss this in private?'

'No, no I need some friendly faces around me' Louise said as she turned and smiled at the two ladies standing behind her.

'Tea, Coffee,' Rachel offered and went to fulfil the requests leaving Jana and Louise with the two men.

Officer Ramos began to speak to Louise in Spanish, 'Por favor, permítanme asegurarles que esto es sólo una formalidad, voy a tratar de mantener las preguntas a un mínimo.'

'Please let me reassure you that this is just a formality, and I will endeavour to keep questions to a minimum' Carlos Interpreted.

'Thank you very much' replied Louise before the questioning proceeded. As the policeman continued questioning, so Carlos continued with the interpretation.

'You are the lady who raised the alarm?' Carlos repeated the question to Louise.

'Yes' said Louise. Carlos continued to interpret further questioning on behalf of the police, as his head moved back and forth between the policeman and Louise, speaking to each one in turn.

'Did you know the deceased personally?' he asked

'Yes, he is my uncle' Louise replied

'We are sorry for your loss,' Carlos said before continuing the questioning.'

'Thank you' Louise replied.

'Had he been in poor health of late' Carlos continued.

'No, he liked to keep himself as active and fit as possible' Louise replied in response.

Following a further conversation with the policeman, Carlos explained more to Louise about Spanish laws and what happens whenever a sudden death occurs. Officer Ramos will need to inform a magistrate who will then make an order for a forensic doctor to perform an autopsy before your uncle's body can be repatriated to the UK.

'I am sorry, but they will have to examine the body, as the death is unexpected,' Carlos said.

'How long will that take? When will I be able to take him home?' Louise said as she began to cry again. Carlos explained a body must be embalmed within forty-eight hours; the autopsy should take place before then. Carlos also explained to her that they would find an English-speaking funeral director who will assist you with the repatriation details and speak to your chosen funeral directors back home. Carlos advised Louise that he would if she wished, support her with all of this. 'would you please Carlos; I think it will be all too much to cope with alone' said Louise

'I will find out all the information that you require first, and then I'll get back to you tomorrow' Carlos promised her as he held out his business card to her.

'Should you need me, I am available on this number, call me anytime'.

'thank you very much' said Louise.

Jana thanked the two men and showed them out. As she walked back into the room, Louise began to sob again, Jana put her arm around her shoulder and speaking softly to Louise said, 'You should not be alone tonight, why don't you stay with me at my apartment? Until your husband arrives tomorrow.' Louise smiled and thanked Jana for her generosity. Time passed quickly; it was five-thirty in the evening. Rachel interrupted the conversation. 'Would you like to get something to eat? You really should eat something.' Rachel had kept quiet when Louise was being questioned by the authorities, only speaking to offer them more refreshments.

'Yes, I agree, you need to keep your strength up' Jana said,

'Seven o'clock, in the restaurant? Rachel said, not waiting for an answer. The police still had Louise's apartment cordoned off although Jana was able to use hers. 'Come on, you can borrow some of my clothes, 'Jana said before they headed off to her apartment. They both showered and changed before heading off to meet Rachel promptly at seven o'clock, at the restaurant. Jana had a bottle of wine brought to the table. 'It's been an exhausting day, I think we could all do with a glass of wine or two,' she said as she looked at Rachel and Louise. Louise nodded and smiled at Jana.

'I can't thank you both enough for your help today.' Louise told them as she held out her hands to hold theirs, they both smiled at Louise.

They continued to chat while waiting for their meal. Jana told them about the stranger in the crowd who had been following her at the market, and how she had been enjoying the afternoon wandering around the stalls, before the stranger had made her feel uncomfortable. Jana explained how a strange man had been popping up on stalls close to her throughout the afternoon and how, when she had sat down, he had come to sit next to her. It had been her arm that he had been staring at, she recalled. Jana had not realised this before now. 'I never used to scare that easy, but that man was making me feel uncomfortable' Jana continued with her story.

'What did you do' Louise asked.

'I went back to the coach.' By now, the waiter had arrived with the food and another bottle of wine that Rachel had ordered. As they began to eat their food, Jana's story got pushed to the back of her mind, and they all ate their meals in silence. When they finished their meal, they all went back into the bar area, the third bottle of wine ordered, they found a table away from the main path of other holidaymakers. Jana hoped that they would get more peace away from the bar. True to her curious ways, Rachel asked Jana to tell them what had happened with the stranger and so the conversation drifted back to Jana's afternoon at the market.

Jana picked up the story where she had left off when their meal had arrived; 'As I said, I went back to the coach, I walked to the coach at a pace, practically running. I kept looking over my shoulder for the strange man' she said.

'Where was he?' Rachel said

'He didn't follow me back to the coach' Jana said as she breathed a sigh of relief.

'Thank heavens for that' Rachel said

'How was your journey back? I would have been too worried to travel alone after that' Louise stated. Jana smiled and remembered the old gentleman on the bus, 'I had my bodyguard' Jana said as she remembered her time with him. Jana continued to tell them about the older man; how friendly he had been and how safe he had made her feel. She proceeded to say to them how George had spoken about his wife, how much love there was for her. He had told her how his wife had passed away two years earlier and the look on his face as he spoke of the love and support that she had given him throughout their time of marriage.

Jana went on to say how he had told her that they had longed for a family of their own and although not being blessed with children of their own, they had a niece who they both adored and felt that she was more of a daughter than a niece to them. Jana told them how she could recall the look of pure love in his eyes when he spoke about his niece, and the sadness in them as he spoke of the regret, he felt of not being able to say goodbye to his niece. Jana recalled the limp and how he had tapped against his leg and the sound it made, like knocking on wood. Louise's pallor changed as she took in what Jana was saying. 'Are you alright' Jana asked Louise. In rapid sequence, Louise then began to throw questions at Jana. 'What time did you speak to him? Do you know his name? Describe what he looked like.' Both Jana and Rachel looked at Louise with concern and confusion on their faces. 'Please answer me' said Louise pleading with Jana. Jana set about answering the questions as accurately and truthfully, as she could remember.

Jana recalled the day; the coach had returned from the market at around noon. Jana began to describe the older gentleman to Louise and Rachel. 'He was a very distinguished-looking gentleman, with thick white hair and no signs of baldness. He told me his name was George' Jana explained to them both. Louise was taken aback by the description that Jana was providing; in disbelief, she asked Rachel to see if it was the man in the photograph and handed her a picture of her uncle to Rachel. Rachel gasped as she realised that the description that

Jana had given was indeed the man in the photograph. Rachel turned over the photo, on the back in tiny writing, there was a message. Rachel read it silently to herself before reading; it allowed for Jana to hear what her auntie and uncle wrote with love for Louise.

#

To our dear Louise,

You have meant more to us than any niece ever could. We have always thought of you as our daughter, as our very own flesh and blood, our very own little girl. We have walked and talked with you, laughed and cried with you. We are so full of pride for you, and this is the proudest moment of our lives; we love you with all our hearts.

Love

Auntie Emily and Uncle George XX

#

Rachel showed Jana the photograph; it was a photo of Louise and her auntie and uncle on Louise's wedding day, Louise had kept the picture in her bag since her auntie had passed away. Jana looked over to Louise, expecting her to fly into a rage, telling Jana that she could not have met her uncle as he had not been alive at that time. Jana and Rachel looked at Louise at the same time; she was crying, she got up and hugged Jana as she looked up to the heavens and said 'Goodbye Uncle George.' Louise turned to Jana and said, 'Thank you, Jana, thank you for telling me goodbye from my uncle. George always said that he would find a way of letting me know he was safe and well on his passing, and through you, he has kept his promise.' Louise then pulled them both towards her, hugging them she said' Total strangers we were when we met, lifelong friends we will remain.' They all lifted their glasses and said, 'To uncle George' and toasted his life and his love. Jana thought back to the day on the bus when she had been chatting to George, that's why the other passengers had been giggling on the bus. They had not been able to see George and so thought Jana had been talking to herself.

They all continued to chat about George and how Louise's life had been growing up with her auntie and uncle around her for some time. Jana then excused herself and went for a walk; her thoughts drifted back to her grandparents and how she enjoyed her holidays with them. Jana decided to take a stroll to the beach. It was a warm night, the breeze off the sea cooled her a little as she got closer to it.

#

The smell of the sea always reminded Jana of shellfish and especially her favourite cockles, Jana began smiling as she remembered her grandfather sitting on the beach with his trousers rolled up around his ankles, eating a tub of muscles and laverbread and her grandmother with a tub of cockles. Would you like to taste one Jana?' her grandmother asked her, holding the container in front of her. 'No, try one of these, they are a lot nicer than cockles' her grandfather said to her as he held out a tub of muscles to her. Unsure which one to try first, Jana closed her eyes and with her grandparents outstretched offerings; she dipped into one of the tubs before putting the seafood into her mouth, she had never been afraid to try something new. Jana had picked out a cockle; she remembered how it tasted and the texture, with the gritty feeling as she chewed on it. Her grandfather then held out the muscles again for her to take one, as Jana put one into her mouth, she began to feel nauseous, spitting out the flesh she said 'yuck, how can you eat them grandad?'

Her grandparents began to laugh; Jana was smiling to herself, even more now, as she recalled her grandmother's smile widening when Jana said she liked the cockles better and would never eat another muscle, 'As long as I live' she said joining her grandparents laughing now. Jana missed her grandparents; her memories of them always made her feel happier and safe.

#

Jana reached the central shopping area by the beach; she walked along the street and began window shopping. She had been drawn to a store the first day that she had arrived on the island, seeing it as she passed by in the taxi on the way to the hotel from the airport. Jana came across the shop, and as she walked in, she could feel the atmosphere change, feeling relaxed, she browsed and there on the shelf stood angel ornaments in various designs and colours. 'Hello, can I help you?' a voice came from behind her, Jana turned to see a woman smiling at her.'

'Yes please, could I look at these angels' replied Jana,

'Certainly, this is a musical one' the woman explained as she reached for an angel. She took it down from the shelf for Jana to have a closer look.

'Do they all play the same music?' Jana asked

'No, there are some that play a different tune' the woman replied, she began to look at the boxes containing angels to see which songs they played. Jana chose three different designs, different music, and various colours. 'Three angels?' The woman had become inquisitive. 'Yes, one for myself and one each for my friends' Jana replied. The woman gave Jana a knowing smile.

'Please permit me to do a reading for you' the woman said

'A reading?' Jana replied puzzled.

'Yes, it will be free of charge to you, I work with the angels, I read angel tarot cards' she explained to Jana.

Jana was intrigued now; she had been to see a psychic when she was at home after she lost her grandparents but had not been impressed by them. Jana agreed to the reading, the woman closed the shop door and turned the closed shop sign around before she showed Jana into the back room. Jana took in the look of the room; the atmosphere was calm and relaxing. She could see a table with a dark purple silk tablecloth and a white candle in a silver candlestick sitting in the centre of it. 'Please sit, my name is Gloria' the woman was now introducing herself to Jana. 'I'm Jana, pleased to meet you' Jana replied. As she sat down, Gloria lit the candle and turned off the ceiling light. As she did so, Jana could see that the room had softer lighting around the walls, this changed the atmosphere of the place, and it became more pleasant. Before Gloria started the reading, Jana felt the need to ask, 'why are you doing this free of charge for me?'

'It is what the angels want of me' replied Gloria,

'You speak to the angels?' Jana enquired

'Yes, since I was a tiny child.' replied Gloria.

Gloria began to explain to Jana how the cards worked and how they would give her guidance and answers. 'The spread that I am going to use is called the Celtic spread' Gloria began. Jana puzzled now; listened carefully, she did not want to miss anything and expressed this to Gloria. 'How will I remember everything that you tell me?' Jana asked.

'With your permission, I will record it for you' Gloria replied.

'Thank you, that would be very nice of you' Jana said. Gloria asked Jana to shuffle the cards and pick out ten of them. As Gloria lay them out on the table in front of her, she smiled and looked up at Jana. 'You have angels with you. We are all given a guardian angel when a child 's life starts in the mother's womb' Gloria said. Jana was about to ask a question when Gloria raised her hand in a gesture to stop her as she continued to speak. 'You called on your angel in a great time of need' Gloria was looking at Jana's arm, again with a knowing look. 'It was not the first time you had called on your angel, it was the most ominous time, and the need for your angel's help and guidance was the greatest at this time' Gloria continued.

Jana could feel the tears running down her face; she did not know why she was crying but felt an overwhelming need. 'The angels ask me to tell you that they have been with you in all of your times of need. 'It was the one time that you had asked for their help' Gloria was now handing Jana a box of tissues, that she had placed on the table beside her, Jana did not recall seeing them on the table or Gloria putting them there. Gloria continued with the reading, 'The angels tell me that you have had a glimpse of the other side, that you have been to the spirit world. They also tell me that you were sent back to us so that you can help others in their times of need.' Gloria paused to look at the cards before continuing with the reading. 'there is a darkness that hangs over you, someone, a man in the shadows. You are very uncomfortable when this man is around. The angels say that you have nothing to fear from this man and that the truth will open up to you when the time is right.' Gloria began to pack up the cards, while at the same time, she explained a little more to Jana.

'You are a fortunate lady, you may not feel lucky right now, but believe me, you are. Not many people of this world can communicate with the angels and spirits as you do, I feel, however, that you have not been receiving spirit for long.' Gloria continued, 'I feel that you have many questions unanswered, would you like a cup of tea or coffee before we tackle them.'

'Yes please, tea would be lovely, that would be so kind of you' replied Jana. They sat down to drink their tea and to tackle some of the questions Jana had been thinking about when there was a knock on the shop door. Gloria excused herself and went to answer it. When she returned to Jana, she apologised, 'I am so sorry Jana, one of my suppliers, has arrived late and won't be able to make the delivery at a different time, I am so sorry, I am going to have to deal with this.'

'I understand, I can come back another day' Jana said. Gloria showed Jana to the door, handing her, her bag of angels that she had purchased earlier and said goodbye.

Jana continued to window shop as she made her way back to the hotel; she headed straight for the lounge, guessing that Rachel and Louise would still be there. Sure enough, there they were with a glass of wine in their hands. 'Well, where have you been?' Rachel asked.

'To get you both a gift' Jana said as she held a bag out to each of them. Jana laughed now as she read the surprise on their faces.

'Angels?' asked Louise puzzled,

'Yes, I think it's time we all had angelic intervention in our lives' replied Jana as she thought back to her guardian angel and how she had first met her.

Jana caught the waiter's eye, 'Could we have a bottle of wine, 'No' some sangria and fresh glasses please' Jana asked as she changed her mind at the last minute.

'With pleasure miss,' the waiter replied with a smile.

'Sangria,' Rachel asked with a puzzled look on her face.

'why not? Something different for a change I think' Jana said.

'Ok' replied Rachel smiling, she could not resist saying 'but it contains wine.'

Louise had been quiet, Jana turned to her with a concerned look on her face. 'Are you alright, Louise?' she asked

'No, I don't feel I should be out drinking and enjoying myself with you, not after uncle George,' Louise replied tearfully

'What would your uncle George be saying to you now? Rachel asked, joining in the conversation. Louise thought for a few seconds before replying, 'he would say, we will be dead soon enough, and life is for celebrating and not mourning' said Louise

'Exactly, that's what we should do, celebrate his life,' Rachel said, Jana smiled in agreement. The sangria arrived at the table, and Rachel proceeded to pour them all a glass. The pianist was playing music in the background. Jana held her drink up in the air, 'To George' she said.

'Uncle George, I hope you are with Auntie Emily,' Louise said with tears rolling down her cheeks

'George, I may have never met you, but I hear you could be a handful when you got started.' Rachel said as she held her glass up. They all began to laugh at what Rachel had said, Louise, laughing with more vigour now as she nodded in remembrance of her uncle's stubbornness.

The women chatted for a while about loved ones who had passed, each sharing memories and crying and laughing recalling each one. Rachel looked at her watch, 'Look at the time it's one forty-five in the morning, time for bed, I think. I had better go before Stuart comes looking for me.' Both Jana and Louise got up to wish Rachel goodnight as they each hugged her in turn. 'Let's go and get a coffee before we go to bed ourselves,' Jana said to Louise and headed back to the apartment. Jana made the coffee, drinking it they continued to chat for a while before going to bed. Jana was only asleep a short while when the dreams began again. She was back in the street; the streetlights were letting off an eerie glow. The car was back, and the two men were still dragging another man into the vehicle. She could hear them shouting and the man begging for his life.

As before, the dream revealed more, and she could now see they were pointing a gun at the man begging for his life. The man with no face had suddenly turned to look at her, only this time he didn't just stand there, he began to run down the street towards her screaming. Jana started to run the other way. She couldn't run; everything was in slow motion, she was moving her legs, but it felt like she was running through thick mud, being unable to lift her legs. Jana was screaming louder now as the faceless man caught up with her, he was holding onto her shoulders and turning her to face him. Jana did not get to see his face as Louise had begun to shake her calling her name 'Jana, Jana, are you ok' she continued to shout at her to wake her up. Jana was trembling when she woke, Louise held her close as Jana sobbed into her shoulder. 'Come on, let's get you a hot drink,' Louise said as she directed Jana to the kitchen

'I'm so sorry' Jana apologised to Louise for sobbing on her shoulder

'there is no apology needed Jana, would you like to tell me about the dream?' Louise replied.

Jana told her how she had been having the dreams since her accident. Jana recalled how they had not started until after she had seen Justin for the last time. 'Do you think something has happened to him?' Jana was asking Louise

'I think; it was the shock of the accident that started the dreams.' Louise said, pouring out a cup of hot tea for Jana.

'Maybe your right' Jana replied as she lifted her cup to her mouth.

'Oh, I should get ready, Joe's plane will be landing in an hour. Are you going to be alright, Jana?' Louise said as could see it was eight-thirty in the morning and she really needed to get ready, or she would be late. 'Yes, you go and get ready' Jana said with a smile. Louise rushed off to the bathroom to shower and change, leaving Jana with her thoughts.

Jana's thoughts drifted off to the reading that she had received the previous night. As she looked over, Jana could see the angels that she had bought sitting on the coffee table where they were left when she brought them back to the apartment for safekeeping. Her eyes wandered over to the angel that she had chosen for herself; there was a glow coming from it, as she looked more closely, she could see that the radiance was getting brighter. The light started to move towards her, getting bigger until it was in front of her. Her guardian angel was standing in front of her again; this time, Jana was not so shocked and was able to talk to her angel without fear. 'Why are you here? Why do I keep seeing you?' Jana asked the angel.

'You have the gift of sight and knowledge, and you have come back to the earth, so you may help others in their hour of need, as I helped you in your hour of need' replied the angel.

Jana looked carefully at the angel, 'I keep having the same message, but I don't understand how I can help? I don't know what to do' said Jana

'When you are needed, you will know what to do, and I will be at your side guiding you, as will your spirit guides and loved ones from the other side' said the angel

'What if I can't? What if I get scared?' Jana said a little flustered.

'Do not be afraid, I will be there by your side just call on me' said the angel

'How should I call you? What should I call you?' Jana asked

'My name will come to you when you least expect it to and unexpectedly' the angel replied as it faded away. Louise came back into the room; she was dressed now ready to go and pick up her husband from the airport. 'Who were you talking to?' she asked looking around the room,

'You would never believe me' Jana replied with a smile

'Oh, Ok, I'm off to get Joe, I hope they allow us into the apartment when we get back' Louise said with a puzzled look on her face.

'Don't worry, you can come back here until they sort it out if it's not ready' Jana reassured Louise.

'You have been so kind and supportive, both you and Rachel, and I mean what I said yesterday, we will be lifelong friends I don't know what I would have done without you two,' Louise said hugging her.

Jana watched as she left the apartment to go to the airport, she knew what Louise was going through, her losses still feeling raw in her own heart. Thinking she would miss breakfast; she was feeling the effects of a hangover after drinking the sangria the night before. Jana decided to go to the beach for a walk. Walking up the beach, thoughts of Callum entered her mind, and Jana wondered how he was doing. Smiling to herself, Jana knew that Callum had been one lucky young man, that day on the beach. Jana thought of Chris now, and how he had supported her in helping his friend, without him, things could have been different, smiling Jana sent them both wishes of wellness into the air. Jana sat down on one of the stone benches on the seafront, looking out over the horizon, *I am going to have to go on a cruise myself one day* ' she thought to herself, as she watched a cruise ship sail past. Jana began to scan the beach, looking at the people around sunbathing and enjoying the activities on offer. Jana started to feel more relaxed, she took off her sandals and walked down to the sea, she could feel the warm sand as the grains passed between her toes. As the sand was going between her toes, she clenched them, trying to keep her balance as she walked towards the sea.

Jana had been paddling in the sea for some time enjoying the coolness as the waves splashed over her feet. She looked around her, at the view set out before her eyes, 'It's such a beautiful place' she thought to herself. Jana could see a man sitting on the bench where she had been earlier; she held her breath as she recognised the man sitting there to be the one from the market. 'What's he doing here? Why is he staring at me?' she thought. Feeling angry, Jana began to walk up the beach, she wanted to confront the man; *How dare he stare at me and scare me like this, why is he following me?'* The thoughts were loud in her head, and Jana began talking to herself as she walked up the beach. The more she thought about the man, the angrier she was becoming. As Jana got closer to him, he got up from the bench and left; he left before Jana could reach him. 'The truth will be opened up to you when the time is right' she could hear Gloria's voice repeating the sentence in her head.

Wiping the sand from her feet and putting her sandals back on, Jana decided to go and see Gloria; there was so much going on that she did not understand, and she needed some answers. Jana reached the shop to find Gloria shutting up. 'Hello there, I was just about to go out to get some lunch, you could join me if you like' she said to Jana as she took on the angry look on her face. 'Is it that time already? Yes, yes I will thank you' Jana replied. They walked a few streets up to one of the local cafés. When they entered the building, Gloria began to speak Spanish to the older woman behind the food counter. Gloria turned and introduced the older woman, 'This is my mother, Maria' Gloria said as she gestured towards the older woman. Gloria's mother smiled and pointed to one of the tables, 'Please take a seat' she said in broken English, before returning to converse with her daughter.

Gloria joined Jana at her table, 'What is the matter? Why are you so angry?' asked Gloria

'How do you know I'm angry?' Jana answered with a question

'I can sense it' she replied

'I saw that strange man again,' Jana told Gloria and continued to tell her all about him. Gloria listened as Jana got the story off her chest when she finished, Gloria was able to talk, knowing that Jana would now be ready to hear and understand the messages that she was receiving. 'You are not naturally an angry person, why do you allow yourself to get angered by this man?' Gloria asked.

'Your right, it usually takes a lot to get me angry. I think it is because of the fear of not knowing why he is following me' Jana replied.

'As time goes by it will be revealed, Gloria said

'I hope so' replied Jana.

'Now what about the questions you have for me? First, tell me about the vision you had this morning,' Gloria said. Jana looked at Gloria in awe, 'How do you know about my vision' she asked. 'that is my gift, but for now, let us deal with your gift' Gloria replied, smiling.

Jana told her about the dreams and the appearance of the angel, 'I don't know anything about this sort of stuff, angels or spirit guides, why me?' Jana said

'some people believe that angels and spirit guides are the same; this is not my belief.' Gloria said, answering her question. 'now let me explain further, you may be surprised at how long you have really been seeing your angels and the spirits.' Gloria said.

Chapter Three:
The Angel Pin

Gloria continued to explain to Jana, 'at conception, a child has a guardian angel; they are there to help and guide us. They are unable to interfere with our lives unless that is, it is not our time to die. We must always ask them for help before they can intervene. Angels are the light of God and love; they come to us in a form that we are comfortable with; this is so that we do not become afraid.' Gloria explained about the angels to Jana.

'Now tell me what is troubling you, Jana?' Gloria said

'Where do I begin?' Jana replied, she went on to tell Gloria about her life; she felt so comfortable around Gloria that she could not help revealing things about herself. She spoke about her parents and grandparents, and how she had been alone since her teenage years, how she had battled through university alone to become a physiotherapist. She told Gloria about how she had met Justin and the accident where she had lost her arm. Her time in the hospital and her first sighting of the angel. 'I tried to tell my friends about the angel, but they laughed and said I was hallucinating after the anaesthesia' Jana continued. 'I have seen the angel again since and a dead man named George.'

Jana went on to tell her about George and Louise. 'Some people find it hard and some people fear the unknown, you must not allow other people's judgement of you to affect your abilities to speak with the angels and spirits. You have been returned to help both those who are living and those in spirit' Jana continued to be amazed by the explanations that Gloria was giving her. Gloria continued,

'There is more to come in the future for you, your abilities to work with the angels and spirit will continue. Sometimes they will make you cry tears of joy, and other times you will cry tears of sadness. It is your destiny, and you must embrace it with open arms' Gloria was firm with her advice to Jana. It was time for Gloria to open the shop back up and as they were getting up to leave the café, Jana went to pay the bill. Maria began waving her arms fiercely, 'No, no' she kept repeating. Jana looked at Gloria, who started to laugh,

'My mother is insistent' said Gloria. Jana turned to Maria and smiled,

'Thank you so much, you are very kind' she said as she shook Maria's hand.

Jana thanked Gloria for all her help when they reached the shop. 'Don't go yet; I have something for you.' Gloria stopped Jana from walking off, intrigued Jana walked into the shop behind her. Gloria handed her a purple coloured satin-lined box, inside the box, was a gold angel pin. 'It is the most beautiful pin I have ever seen, thank you' Jana said as she opened the box, she reached over and hugged Gloria, 'thank you, thank you' she repeated.

'I have one similar, when I first started talking to angels, I would touch the pin to call on my angels when I needed them,' Gloria said.

'I will remember that' replied Jana. She waved goodbye to Gloria as she went out through the shop door. Smiling to herself, she walked back to the hotel, her thoughts on everything that Gloria had told her.

Jana arrived at the hotel, and walked up past the pool to her apartment, as she entered the room, she found a letter on the floor, the message was barely legible.

#

Jana,

Carlos came to see me, to say that they have completed uncle George's autopsy. I am going to see uncle George this afternoon to say goodbye, if you are back in time, I would like it if you would come with me.

Please meet me at the reception at five o'clock this evening.

Louise X

#

Jana looked at her watch. It was four twenty-five, she rushed to change her clothes into something more suitable and headed for the reception. Louise was there alone; it was apparent her friend was upset. 'Are you alright Louise' Jana said as she sat next to her.

'Oh, thank the heavens you are here, I didn't think you would make it. I have asked Rachel to join us as well. I know you both had never met uncle George, well not when he was alive' she smiled at Jana. 'I thought you might both like to be able to meet him; you have both been so supportive, and I know uncle George would have liked you both' Louise said. 'Hi, you two' Rachel had joined them now, Stuart is waiting outside to take us to see George 'she said. In the car, they chatted about irrelevant and meaningless topics, to help distract them all from the task ahead. Carlos met them at the main doors; he hugged Louise before they went in. Inside the Chapel of Rest, Carlos spoke to the undertaker who had been organised to take care of George.

The undertaker showed them into a room where George lay in his coffin. 'I will be in the other room if you need me' Carlos said as he left the three women inside.

'Thank you' Jana said, and Carlos left the room closing the door behind him. Louise went over to George.

'It looks like he's sleeping, he looks at peace. I can almost see a smile on his face' said Louise as she kissed him on the forehead.

'That is because he is smiling' Jana replied. Louise and Rachel looked at her and found that Jana was looking towards the corner of the room and smiling.

'What do you mean? Louise asked. Jana looked at the two women then back to the corner of the room. 'George is here; he wants you to know that he is not in the coffin and that what you are looking at is only the vessel that held his soul. Yes, Louise, he is with your aunt Emily, she is here with him now. Your aunt asked me to tell you that your uncle did not die alone and that indeed she had been there with him, as she would have been if she had been on the earth when he passed.'

Both Louise and Rachel were crying, through the tears, Louise asked, 'How do you know this Jana?' 'It's a long story, I promise I will tell you about it later, but for now, you need to say goodbye to George and Emily it is time for them to go. George instructs that you see his solicitor back home. They want you to know how much you are loved and want me to remind you that you are a daughter to them.' Jana turned to the corner of the room again and smiling she said, 'You are more than welcome George.' Jana turned back to her friends, Louise, please look, into the corner.' Jana said and pointed to the corner she wanted her to look at. Louise did as she asked with Rachel mirroring her. The tears flowed harder down each of the women's faces as they saw a glimpse of George and Emily waving goodbye to them. They turned back to the coffin, and each one kissed George goodbye before leaving.

Carlos was talking to the undertaker as they left the room, he advised Louise of the arrangements made for George's burial. A flight had been arranged to take him back home in the next three days, the local undertaker at home had been instructed to pick up his body at the airport, he was to take him directly to the chapel of rest, where other relatives and friends will have a chance to say goodbye to uncle George. Carlos also reassures Louise that Georges insurance would cover all the costs and that he had arranged for Louise and Joe's plane tickets to go back to the UK at the same time as George. Louise felt relieved by this; she had wondered how she would have found the money to cover the cost. Louise hugged Carlos as she thanked him for all his help, they all said their goodbye and headed back to the car.

The drive back to the hotel went in silence, their thoughts were all on that they had experienced in the room George was in at the chapel of rest. Jana thought about how easy she had received the message from George and Emily and the look on Louise and Rachel's face as she was giving the message. Rachel and Louise were trying to understand how they could have seen George and Emily, and they were both feeling quite shocked, trying to think about how it happened. On their arrival back at the hotel, the manager called Jana over to speak to her. 'There has been a gentleman here to see you today when I advised him that you were not in the hotel, he left his card and asked that I ensured you received it' the manager said in broken English.

'Thank you' Jana said as she took the card from him, she read it as she walked through to the bar. 'Richard Wilson; private investigator' Jana read aloud

'Who is that? What is a private investigator looking for you for' Rachel asked?

'I don't know' Jana replied as she ordered a drink for them all at the bar.

They found a table to sit at overlooking the pool, as they did so, Joe came across the side of the swimming pool and spotting them through the window and waved as he entered into the bar area. 'Hi,' he said, smiling as he bent down to kiss Louise on the cheek. Louise introduced Joe to Jana and Rachel. 'Jana there was a fellow here looking for you, he asked me some questions about you, I told him that I did not know you and that if he had any questions, he should be asking you directly.'

'Thank you, Joe, what did he look like?' Jana asked. Joe thought for a moment before answering.

'He was slim in build, short dark hair, he was not a local he had an accent, American I think' said Joe.

'Do you know who he is?' Rachel asked.

'No, I don't know who he is, what I do know is that he is the man that has been following me around. He is starting to make me feel angry' Jana said with a stern voice.

Stuart arrived, and he was quickly introduced to Joe; they hit it off immediately and headed for the bar together. The women could hear them laughing at the bar, Rachel shouted over to Stuart to get the drinks in. Turning to Jana, Rachel inquisitive as ever began to question her about her ability to speak to the spirit. Jana was unable to answer this question as she could not explain it. Jana did, however, tell both Rachel and Louise about the accident and her first angel visit. She was open and honest when she said to them that she could not explain why she had been given the gift of knowledge and sight, as the angel had told her.

Jana went on to tell them about her visit to the spirit world and how grateful she had felt having seen her father, mother and grandparents again, even if it was for a short while. Jana was sullen now as she told them of her coming back, away from her family and how she did not want to live, she did not want to return to the earth. Jana explained that it was new to her and that she could not find the right words to describe it but promised she would try. 'Can you call a spirit to you?' Rachel asked

'No, they come to me when they need my help.' Jana replied.

'How I don't understand? Do they talk to you? How do you see them? Rachel began to throw the questions hard and fast at Jana. Jana tried to explain the best she could, feeling pressured from Rachel to answer the questions. 'Yes, I see them, they appear as a solid mass to me. I don't know; sometimes I have a black and white vision in my head. I hear them speak, but I don't see their lips move and sometimes I have dreams. It was Louise's turn to ask the questions. 'Is that what happened the other night, the dream I mean?' Louise said

'Yes, that dream has been haunting me since the accident, I don't understand what the meaning of the dream is or what I am supposed to do with what it is revealing to me' Jana replied.

'How did we see my aunt and uncle, at the funeral parlour?' Louise asked

'Honestly, I don't know. What I do know is that for that moment in time, you had a glimpse of spirit.' Jana made a mental note to ask Gloria.

'Please, can we talk about something else, all I can say is that the angel told me I am here to help others. When they need me' Jana ended the conversation sharply she was beginning to get a headache.

A male voice came from behind Jana. 'Well, well, you're a hard woman to catch up with.' Jana turned to see the man who had been following her, as he came to stand beside her. He was looking down at her, she stood up abruptly and stepping back fell backwards over the leg of the chair, bumping her head on the corner of the table behind her.

'Jana, Jana!' Rachel was screaming her name

'Joe, call an ambulance and the police.' Louise shouted over to him. People were running around everywhere as Jana lay unconscious on the floor. When the ambulance arrived, Jana was still unconscious, the paramedics busied themselves and got her into the ambulance as quickly as they could. Rachel and Louise followed the ambulance to the hospital and sat in the family room, waiting for news on Jana. The doctors were in with Jana; they had both tried to talk to the doctors but had difficulty with the language barrier. Rachel rang Carlos and asked if he would help them.

Carlos arrived at the hospital to find them wheeling Jana out of the room. He spoke to the doctor for a short while before speaking with Rachel and Louise. 'They are taking Jana to the theatre, there is a bleed on the brain, and they have to operate immediately.' Carlos informed the girls about what was happening.

'Is she going to be alright?' Rachel asked as she broke down in tears.

'We should call her family' Carlos replied

'I don't think she has any family still alive' Louise said

'Then we shall be here for her' Rachel said as she pulled herself together.

'Let's go and get a coffee, there is not much we can do here but wait for now' Carlos suggested. Jana recognised that she was in the hospital theatre as she found herself to be floating over her body again, her angel by her side reassuring her that all would be well.

What seemed like hours for Rachel and Louise felt like seconds for Jana, and she was again returning to her body. Jana was taken to the high dependency ward and remained unconscious when Rachel and Louise could visit her there. Carlos was in conversation with the doctor who did the operation, and he said that Jana would be unconscious for some time, as they had to remove the pressure to the brain from the bleed.

Carlos returned to the two women and explained this to them. He also advised that they go back to the apartments to let Jana rest. Rachel demanded to know what was happening to the man who had caused the accident. Carlos promised that he would speak to the police and get back to them. They returned to the hotel as advised by Carlos, they had decided against having a meal; they did not feel hungry and continuously worried about Jana.

'I hope she is alright' Rachel said, beginning to cry again.

'She will be, she's a fighter. She had been through a lot worse than this' Louise said

'Hello ladies' it was Carlos, he was smiling at them. 'I have spoken to the hospital and Jana is awake. They are going to keep her in the hospital for a few days to monitor her.' Rachel and Louise jumped up and hugged each other before turning to hug Carlos.

Carlos began to laugh, 'Jana would like you to take some of her clothing and toiletries to her, the doctors have asked if you could do that in the morning so that she can rest tonight.'

'Of course,' Rachel said

'What about that, man?' asked Louise, her thoughts turning to what had happened. Carlos explained that he had contacted the police 'They have been questioning him for some hours. He has been hired to find the woman who saved some young man's life on the beach' Carlos said.

'I remember that day; they said the woman had vanished' Rachel said.

'Why would they be searching for her?' Louise asked.

'The family want to thank her in person' Carlos said.

'I don't understand, why would a private detective follow someone openly? He must have known that he was scaring Jana,' Rachel replies angrily as she waved for the waiter to come over with fresh coffee.

'I am sorry, I don't know the answer to that' Carlos said. He excused himself, promising that he would catch up with them in the morning.

The following morning Rachel and Louise took Jana her things as promised. Jana had been in and out of consciousness throughout the night, but when they arrived, she was sitting up in bed. Jana smiled at them, and when they got closer, they saw the bruise running down the side of her face. 'Thank heavens, you are here, it will be nice to be able to have a chat, no one speaks English here' Jana said, smiling at them both.

'How are you feeling?' Rachel asked

'I have a headache, and I'm aching. I'm ok' Jana replied smiling

'I'm not surprised, have you seen the bruise on the side of your face?' Louise said, handing Jana a mirror. Jana looked at the bruise on her face; it did indeed look nasty. She could only see the side of her face as bandages covered her head. 'I promise, it is not as bad as it seems, Jana lied to reassure Rachel and Louise who both looked at her with disbelief.

'Do you remember what happened?' Rachel asked

'Yes, that man who has been following me was there, wasn't he?' Jana said

'Yes, apparently, he is a private detective, and he has been looking for you' Louise said as Rachel nodded her head.

'Why? What does he want?' Jana asked. Rachel was about to answer when the doctor entered the room with Carlos.

Carlos spoke to Rachel and Louise, 'could you excuse us, ladies, please, the doctor would like to check how Jana is doing' Carlos said, smiling.

'We will be in the canteen, please come and fetch us when he has finished' Rachel said

'Of course,' Carlos replied. Rachel and Louise bent over to hug Jana before leaving the room.

'Good morning' the doctor said to Jana in broken English before continuing in Spanish. Carlos explained that the doctor would need to assess her injuries before he could decide whether to discharge her from the hospital. 'I will be just outside the door' Carlos said as a nurse walked into the room. Jana smiled at Carlos as he left the room; she was feeling very nervous and scared. With the doctor's assessment over, Carlos came back into the room. Carlos interpreted what the doctor said to Jana. He could feel Jana's hurt as he told her that the doctor wanted to keep her in the hospital longer, 'just to make sure you are well' he said. Carlos told Jana that they would be moving her to another ward. 'The doctor wants you to remain in the hospital for the rest of the week.'

Jana began to cry; it had been hard enough for her when she was in the hospital at home. Here no one could speak English, and to make matters worse, she had been placed in a side room on her own. This had left her to feel as if a dark cloud was hanging over her. Carlos could not bear to see her crying and leaving her, went to get Rachel and Louise. Carlos was running, he knew it was wrong to run in the hospital and that he shouldn't run, but Carlos needed to get to Rachel and Louise as fast as he could, Carlos had never seen a woman cry so hard. Rachel and Louise stood up as he entered the canteen, their hearts beating as they realised something was wrong. Breathless Carlos tried to explain, the women looked at him blankly then one after the other began to run to the ward, without explanation. They reached Jana's room, and there was no sign of her.

They turned towards the nurse's station to find that there was a body being pushed by two hospital porters to the hospital morgue. They were both unable to stop themselves crying, believing the body to be that of Jana's, they held on to each other.

A nurse was trying to explain to them what was happening without success; Carlos entered the ward and began a conversation with the nurse. Rachel and Louise were listening carefully, shaking their heads as they waited for information on what was happening. Carlos turned from the nurse to face them. He calmly explained that Jana was in the shower and that she was well, and they were asked to go into Jana's room to wait.

Here Carlos was able to explain why he had been rushing to them; they began to laugh at themselves. 'I have always been impatient; I shall have to learn to wait and listen' Rachel said. Again, they both began to hug each other, as they did so, Jana entered the room, 'Are you alright?' Carlos asked.

'Yes, you gave us a fright' Rachel said, and Louise explained to Jana what had happened, they all began to laugh. 'Nothing that drastic, they need to keep me in for a while to make sure that there are no further problems.' Jana said. Carlos excused himself, and they all hugged him before he left. 'thank you, Carlos' Jana said as she hugged him and with a smile he was gone.

'I'm sorry I frightened you both. It's just the thought of being stuck in this hospital with no one I can converse with' Jana said

'Yes, that's a nuisance' Louise said

'Don't worry we shall be here every day' Rachel said

'I am so sorry, Jana; I can't make that promise. I will be taking uncle George home the day after tomorrow.' Louise said.

'I had been hoping that I could come with you, I am sorry to let you down.' Jana said with a tear in her eyes.

'Don't be sorry, you have done everything that you possibly could to help George and me. Louise said

'How long are you staying in Lanzarote?' Rachel asked Jana

'I should be going home by the end of next week. I don't know what's going to happen until I'm released from the hospital' Jana replied. Louise left the room without explanation.

Jana and Rachel followed her with their gaze before returning to look at each other. Rachel shrugged her shoulders, and they chatted about everyday things. They were both worried about Louise, she had been gone for some time. 'Would you like a cold drink?' Rachel asked Jana, trying to distract her from her worries.

'Yes please, that would be nice, thank you.'

'I won't be long' Rachel said with a smile as she left to go to the hospital shop to get them. While she was gone, Louise returned with Joe. 'Hi Jana, hope you are getting well' Joe said as he bent to kiss her cheek.

'Thank you, Joe, yes, I am. I just need to get out of here.' Jana replied

'Speaking of getting out of here, Joe has been talking to uncle George's solicitor back home. Uncle George has left me everything as I was his only living relative, including the apartment, and we both would like you to stay at the apartment, for a long as you want Jana,' Louise said. Jana became overwhelmed by the offer, and the tears began to run down her face, Jana had not wanted to return to the UK just yet, she felt she had a lot to learn from Gloria, she would have gone for Georges funeral and returned to Lanzarote after that.

At that moment, Rachel came back into the room and as nosy as ever asked what was going on. Jana told her all about the offer that Louise and Joe had made. 'That's great, now I have company. Stuart has had to go home, there is something wrong with work' Rachel told them. Turning to Louise, she asked if she would be returning anytime soon. 'I hope so, I just have to say goodbye to uncle George, maybe I could come back for a while after that' Louise replied, looking up at her husband. Joe smiled and nodded in reply to her unspoken question.

'We have to go; we have to get our things packed. First, let me give you my mobile and house numbers.' Louise said before she and Joe said goodbye to Jana and Rachel. Rachel handed Jana her cold drink and stayed with Jana until she was told to leave. She promised Jana that she would return tomorrow' the doctors are going to discharge you quicker than you think, they are going to get sick of the sight of me. See you tomorrow' she said laughing. The hospital porters came to take her to her new ward, she had been placed in an eight-bedded unit. Jana still felt as if she was on her own, no one else could speak English. Feeling exhausted, Jana laid down and went to sleep.

It was not long before she was dreaming, the same dream, the same men only this time two men were chasing her and not one as in her other dreams before. Jana woke to find nurses around her, she had been screaming out in her sleep. One nurse sat beside her comforting her the best way she could, the other left the ward and returned a short while later with a cup of tea when Jana was more relaxed, they went to see to other patients. Jana lay awake, thinking about her dream and what it could mean. The one thing that she did understand from the nightmare was that the second man in it represented the private detective who had been following her. Jana still felt uncomfortable about the man despite knowing that he was a private detective. She was unable to rationalise why she felt that way, but it was a deep feeling in the pit of her stomach. Jana remembered what Gloria had taught her about asking the angels for help. She called on her angel and asked for comfort so that she could sleep soundly that night. As she did so, Jana felt a warm feeling around her as if being hugged softly, she fell asleep shortly after.

Jana began dreaming again, the dream was different this time. Jana was back on the beach with her grandparents tasting the cockles and muscles. This time Jana felt as though she was looking at the dream from a different position as if she was watching someone else and not herself. As she continued to watch, she saw a familiar light, she knew it was her angel. Jana was smiling in her sleep now, it made her feel safe and secure to know that her angels had been with her at such a young age. The remainder of Jana's sleep that night was peaceful and relaxing. Nurses had been back and forth doing their rounds of the patients, checking their clinical observations and ensuring that their patients were safe. Jana had not felt the nurses lifting her arm to take her blood pressure or placing the tympanic in her ear to check her temperature. She slept soundly and solidly.

Jana woke the following morning to the sun shining in the window beside her bed, she sat up to look out of the window. It was a glorious day, it helped Jana's spirits to lift, smiling, she made a promise to herself. Jana vowed not to allow anyone to scare her in that way again Jana was looking forward to seeing the private detective again if only to give him a piece of her mind. A nurse came to her bedside to tell her that the porters had come to fetch Jana for a second x-ray to her head following instruction from the doctor. When she arrived back to the ward, they were bringing lunch around. Jana had just finished her meal when Carlos walked in. Smiling, Jana asked why he was there. 'I could not leave you in my country alone,' Carlos replied with a smile. I asked the doctor to let me know when he would be speaking to you so that I could be here to translate for you. I hope you don't mind, besides my wife would never forgive me leaving one of her countrywomen stranded.' Carlos said, laughing, and Jana began to laugh with him.

'No, I am very grateful, thank you' Jana said.

Carlos sat with her for a while before the doctor came and told her all about his wife and children and how he had met his wife by interpreting for her. Just then, the doctor came, and Carlos explained the conversation for her. 'I heard you had a bad night' the doctor said.

'Just a dream, I've had them for quite some time' Jana replied

'Would you like to discuss it with me?' the doctor asked.

'No thank you, I'm used to having them now' Jana replied. She did not feel the need for the doctor to be poking around in her mind. What I do want to know is 'when I can get out of here' she said a little irritable. The doctor asked Carlos to leave while he examined Jana and called him back in when he finished.

Carlos was called back when the doctor finished, and following a small discussion between Carlos and the doctor, Carlos turned to Jana. 'Do you have someone you can stay with?'

'Yes, I can stay with Rachel,' Jana said with her fingers crossed. Carlos repeated this to the doctor, who gave further instructions to Carlos. Carlos was firm when he told Jana that under no circumstances was she to drink alcohol as the medications the doctor was giving her to take home with her would have a reaction to it should she drink while on them, advising her that the doctor had said it would make her extremely ill. Jana promised not to drink alcohol and asked if she could go. The doctor nodded and shaking her hand, told her that she could be discharged, he then said his goodbye to them both.

Carlos offered to bring her back to the apartment, refusing to take no for an answer. 'After all, I saw you cross your fingers' he said, and I want to ensure that you would be staying with Rachel. Jana did not have a choice but to agree. Carlos had the manager ring Rachels apartment and to Jana's dismay refused to let her go anywhere until he had spoken to Rachel. Carlos left instructions to meet them in the bar area. While they waited, Carlos made Jana promise to follow the doctor's instructions. 'Hello, I wasn't expecting you to come back yet.' Rachel said when she saw Jana with Carlos. 'The doctor was surprised at how remarkably well she has healed,' Carlos said, looking at Jana. 'What do you mean?' Jana asked

'Well, the doctor felt sure that there was a fracture as well as a bleed, as it showed up on the first x-ray. When he checked the second x-ray, however, there was no sign of the fracture, he believes it to be a miracle.' Carlos said, smiling. Jana also laughed, but to herself, Jana knew that this could only be the work of the angels and sent a silent thank you up to them.

Carlos continued to tell Rachel of the agreement made between Jana and the doctor. 'Jana has to have someone she could stay with, and she must not drink alcohol' Carlos said.

'I will be alright on my own' Jana said

'Oh no, you don't, you will stay with me, to be honest, I could do with the company' Rachel said.

'Good that's settled then, I shall bid you farewell for now' Carlos said, giving a little bow to them before leaving.

'Right, let's get you settled; would you like something to eat before we go up to the apartment?' Rachel asked

'Yes, please, I ate very little at the hospital. I didn't know what they were giving me' Jana said.

'You had better phone Louise and let her know how you are and that you are staying with me for a while, just in case she phones the hospital to see how you are' Rachel said. Doing as she was told Jana phoned Louise and was pleased to hear her voice. All too soon, the meal had arrived, and she had to say goodbye, Louise promised to call her in the morning.

Jana and Rachel chatted over their lunch, 'have you seen that detective?' Jana asked.

'No and I'd better not, is all I can say after what he did to you' Rachel said with venom in her tone. Jana laughed, and they continued with their meal before going to the apartment. Jana called into her apartment to collect some of her stuff on the way to the Rachels apartment, she would have to return tomorrow to get the rest. There was no point leaving her stuff there, she would be moving into Louise's apartment as soon as she could. *"I am going to have to settle the bill for my apartment in the morning, "* Jana thought to herself.

Sitting on the veranda, Jana looked out over the ocean, 'you have a beautiful view of the sea from here' she shouted to Rachel as she took in the view of the sun setting over the horizon. Rachel had been the bed in the spare room, she then made coffee and took a cup out to Jana. Rachel found her sleeping on the sunbed. Tiptoeing back in Rachel left Jana to rest. Rachel rang Louise and reassured her that Jana was safe, she promised to look after Jana and told Rachel that she would be staying with her until she was well enough to be on her own. Louise thanked her for letting her know' it's such a relief to know she is in safe hands,' Louise said before hanging up the phone. The three of us have become good friends, Rachel said to herself before joining Jana on the sunbed next to her on the veranda. Soon Rachel had also fallen asleep.

They both woke to the phone ringing, it was Stuart. He was ringing to see how his wife was and to update her on the problems back home. 'How is Jana?' Stuart asked.

'She's getting there, I'll look after her' Rachel replied.

'Hi, Stuart' Jana shouted from the veranda. Jana looked out over the sea, she could see a cruise liner passing and wondered what it was like onboard. Rachel had finished her call with Stuart, and she joined Jana back on the veranda. 'have you ever been on a cruise liner?' Jana asked her as she continued to watch the liner cruise along. Rachel watched her for a while before answering, wondering what was going on in Jana's head. 'No, I never thought about it really, why?' said Rachel.

'It's something I would like to do someday' replied Jana shrugging her shoulders.

'Shall we go down and watch the entertainment, if you feel up to it' Rachel asked Jana changing the subject.

'That would be good, I could do with being entertained' Jana replied.

'Good, no alcohol for you, doctor's orders' Rachel reminded Jana before they left to go down to the entertainments lounge.

As they watched the show, Jana began to relax, she knew she would have to take it easy and stay with Rachel for a few weeks until she was well enough to be on her own. Jana sat back and listened to the music, tapping her fingers on the table in unison to the beat, she put her thoughts aside. Jana planned to enjoy the night and was grateful for Rachels company. They watched the entertainment until it was over and then headed back to the apartment. Coffee was made, and they went onto the veranda to drink it. It was a warm night, and they hoped the fresh air would cool them down a little. They chatted into the early hours, talking about their favourite film stars and who they would marry. Laughing and giggling like schoolgirls made the time pass by quickly and before they knew it was three-thirty am. They said goodnight to each other before going to bed. Rachel made sure that Jana was asleep and settled before she went to bed herself. Jana may have been acting like she was feeling alright, but it had been evident to Rachel the amount of pain Jana had been in. Rachel saw that Jana was unable to stop the cringes from reaching her face every time the pain hit.

Rachel scanned Jana's room to make sure the window was shut, as she did so she saw Jana's prosthetic arm. She had been used to seeing Jana without her false arm when she was in the hospital but seeing it laying there on Jana's bedside cabinet, made her feel uneasy. Rachel closed the door, walking into her own room her concerns for Jana weighed heavy on her mind. Rachel laid on her bed for a while worrying about Jana, they had not been friends for long, but that made no difference to Rachel, she had become very fond of both Jana and Louise in the short time that she had known them. Rachel was not much older than Jana but vowed to protect and look after her as if Jana was one of her own. Rachel decided in her own mind to speak to Jana about the accident and the private detective in the morning. Turning off the light, she pondered on what she would say to Jana and was soon asleep herself.

Chapter Four:
A New Soul

Jana remained in bed for some time during the morning after being up so late, this prompted Rachel to check on her as it was past ten o'clock and Jana would usually be up between six and seven o'clock. She was sound asleep; her breathing was relaxed and soft. Rachel closed the door gently as not to wake her. She took herself to the veranda with a book and cold drink to wait for Jana to wake up. It was almost noon before Jana woke. Jana got herself showered and dressed before joining Rachel on the veranda. She could smell the coffee that Rachel had made, she said good morning before sitting down on the sunbed next to her.

'Good morning, sleepyhead' Rachel said laughing. Jana could not prevent a yawn from coming, the tears ran down her cheeks as she yawned.

'Goodness is that the time? Why didn't you wake me?' Jana said.

'You looked so peaceful, and you certainly need the sleep' Rachel said.

'I'm going to go for a walk after having my coffee' Jana said

'Not on your own young lady' said Rachel.

'Yes, mother' Jana said and began to laugh with Rachel.

Jana knew that Rachel was only looking out for her safety, secretly she liked having someone worry about her, it made her feel safe, she had not felt this safe in a long time. After they had their coffee and cleaned up, they headed out to the reception.

The manager smiled at them both as they passed, soon they were walking down the slope to the shops. 'Do you mind if I look around the shops while we are here?' Rachel asked

'Of course not, I'd like to look around as well' Jana said with a smile. Jana slowed her pace as she walked, Rachel thought Jana appeared to be preoccupied. Rachel watched her nodding and smiling and wondered why Jana was acting so oddly, she said nothing and just watched Jana as she continued with what she was doing. As they were outside one of the local restaurants, Rachel sat down and ordered two coffees, Jana as if automatically sat down at the table beside her. Jana soon snapped out of it, turning to Rachel she said 'You had better make that your last caffeine intake and no more alcohol for you either. Jana began laughing at the expression on Rachel's face 'What?' Rachel said confused as to what was happening with Jana.

'I don't know how to tell you; I don't want you to become frightened' Jana said, still smiling.

'Oh, just spit it out' Rachel said, she was not one to pussyfoot around, and she was becoming impatient.

Jana looked at Rachel for a while before saying, 'Ok, please allow me to finish before you say anything, I have been judged so many times, I don't know if I could cope with being judged by you right now.'

'I would never judge you, Jana, I may question you, but I would never judge you. Rachel reassured her. The waiter had brought their coffee, and after asking if there was anything else, he could do for them, left them to chat.

'What happened Jana? I watched you, and you seemed to be in a world of your own.' Rachel asked.

'No, not in a world of my own, but I was sharing this one at the time.

'What do you mean?' Rachel said.

'You promise to let me finish.' Jana said.

'I promise, I promise.' Rachel said eagerly.

'I was speaking to my angel. There was a little girl with my angel, the little girl told me that she knew you and that you would know her from a long time ago. I asked her how old she was, and the little girl told me that she would have been seven years old next May, had she lived, she said her given name on earth was Catherine.' Rachel gasped but kept quiet as Jana continued to explain what was happening to her.

As Jana continued, she could see tears running down Rachel's face, this made Jana want to stop giving the message. Jana looked up at her angel,' you must keep going Jana, Catherine has been trying to talk to her mother for some time.' The angel instructed Jana to continue. Smiling Jana looked at Catherine and continued to pass on the message to her mother for her.

'Catherine tells me that it was you who named her and that she had been cruelly taken away by a lump in her brain. Catherine is smiling now and tells me that her life lasted for six hours and even though new-born babies are not supposed to see clearly for some time, she remembers the faces of her mother and father as she looked up into them. Catherine tells me that you are her mother.' Tears were streaming down Rachel's face as she smiled, leading Jana to believe that it was tears of joy, and this made Jana feel a little better. 'Catherine tells me that she loves you and that she has been trying to get your attention for the past ten weeks. That you loved her then and that you love her now, she wants you to know she feels that love, but you need to place that love elsewhere.' It was Jana's turn to have tears as she listened to what Catherine was saying.

Jana was finding it difficult to continue but could see the look on Rachel's face and knew she had to. 'Catherine tells me that there is a new life coming and that the new soul has chosen you and Stuart to be its parents. She wants you to know that you have nothing to fear and that she will be looking after the new life until it is her time to hand that little life over to you. Catherine is laughing as she says she calls it a new life, so as not to spoil it for you.' Jana looked back at her angel and nodded before continuing.' Rachel, Catherine is telling me you must give up the alcohol and caffeine, and my angel agrees with her. Catherine says she must go now, she has a lot of work to do to look after the new life. She wants you to know that the love for you both was and is very strong and she dearly wants you to look out for the signs she has been sending you.' Jana nodded and smiled as she said goodbye.

Looking at Rachel, Jana smiled and said, 'I would offer to get you a drink, but you're not allowed any.' Rachel just stared at Jana; she was still taking in what had been said. Rachel felt the need to question Jana urgently. 'I'm sorry Jana if my questions seem as if I am judging you, please believe me I'm not, I could surely do with a drink right now'. 'How do you know all this? I've never told you about the baby, and I know that Stuart would not have told you.' Rachel asked.

'I find this difficult to explain, I will try my best to make it as understandable as possible for you.' Jana replied.

'Thank you.' Rachel said, the message still going around in her head.

'Let's finish up here, I think you need to go and get yourself a pregnancy test, I feel you are still in doubt.' Jana said. They found a shop and Rachel purchased two pregnancy tests, after all, she had to make sure.

The doctors had told Rachel that she could never have any more children as they would inherit the same birth defect as Catherine. They had advised Rachel against becoming pregnant again if she did, it was imperative that they do a physical health check on her immediately and warned that as a precaution. Informing her that the family doctor's surgery would make a referral back to them straight away.

With the pregnancy tests safely in her bag, Rachel and Jana rushed back to the apartment as fast as their legs could take them. It was when they got back, that Rachel admitted her fears to Jana. 'Let's not worry too soon, let's get these tests done, we will know in what direction to go following the result, ok.' Jana reassured her. Rachel went to do the tests, while she was gone, Jana called upon her angel. 'Why would I be given such a message to give to someone I love, if it is a message of despair.' Jana asked.

'Little one it is not for us to question; I assure you that this child has chosen its own pathway and that pathway does not end at its birth here on earth. The child will see many suns and moons until it comes to the end of its life journey when it will then return to the spirit world from where it came.' The angel had only just finished talking and disappeared when Rachel came out of the bathroom. Rachel was crying and laughing, her emotions all over the place.

Both tests had shown positive, she was scared. Jana could see this and tried to reassure her that everything was going to be ok.

'How do you know Jana?' Rachel asked fearfully.

'I know because my angel has said so, I have faith in my angels not to guide me wrong' Jana said hugging her.

'Now there is one more person who needs to know.' Jana was smiling as she handed the phone over to Rachel.

'I'm worried Jana, I don't know how Stuart is going to take it, he was hurt just as much as I was when we lost Catherine.' Rachel said.

'Well you're not going to be able to hide it for long, and I am sure he will be pleased.' Jana reassured her. Jana waited while Rachel spoke to Stuart, pacing impatiently for Rachel while she gave him the news.

Rachel returned to the room; she had the biggest smile on her face that Jana had seen. Rachel excitedly told her how Stuart had been so happy to hear the news and how he had reassured her that they would get the best medical help they could. Rachel explained how Stuart had taken out private health insurance which will help with her pregnancy. Jana hugged Rachel, before telling her she needed to lay down as she could feel one of her headaches coming on. After taking some medication for the pain, Jana went to her room to lay down, after what seemed like hours Jana was sleeping. Jana woke to find her headache gone, she was pleased for Rachel and Stuart and pleased that she was the one who had been able to pass on the message about the unexpected news. While sleeping, Jana had dreamt of the private detective, the dream had been less frightening than it had been during the night. Jana was beginning to feel a little more comfortable around the subject of the strange man. Jana still thought she needed to give him a piece of her mind and hoped that she had the privilege to do so soon.

After freshening up, Jana found Rachel in the kitchen. Rachel handed a can of cold drink to Jana. Then they sat and chatted for a while, Jana was telling her about the dream when she was distracted by her phone, she heard the alarm go off, she picked it up and read the message, it was a reminder for an appointment.

'Is everything ok?' Rachel asked.

'Yes, I have an appointment to get my prosthesis serviced, it has to be done once every twelve months.' Jana replied.

'When do you have to go?' Rachel said

'Next week, I forgot about it, to be honest' Jana said as she got up to go.

'I'd better go and get dressed; I'll need to arrange a flight back to the UK to get it checked.' Jana said. She went to take a shower before contacting the airport to arrange a flight. Rachel could hear her chatting on the phone, Jana sounded as if she knew the person she was talking to. As inquisitive as ever Rachel could not resist asking Jana about the phone call.

Jana explained that it was one of her old colleagues and that she would have the prosthesis checked at the hospital she used to work in. 'Oh, what did you do at the hospital?' Rachel asked, continuing to be nosey. Jana explained that she had been a physiotherapist before the accident. 'so, you worked at the hospital then, my goodness, it was you at the beach that day, you were the one who saved that young man's life? They said there was something wrong with the woman's arm' Rachel said as she suddenly connected the dots.

'Please, I don't want to think about it, things could have been so different.' Jana said in desperation. Rachel had other ideas and continued to question Jana until she had told her everything. 'That's why that private detective has been looking for you, it's you the family want to thank.' Rachel continued. She would not leave the subject drop and asked Jana what she was going to do about the private detective.

'Ignore him, I really don't need to have that all dragged back up' Jana said.

'Well, you may want to forget all about him, I don't think it will be so easy for you.

Private detectives don't come cheap, so whoever is looking for you is certainly going to great lengths to thank you.' Rachel said with determination in her voice, Jana shuddered at the thought of seeing the private detective again, even though she wanted to give him a piece of her mind.

Jana began to rub the back of her arm at the point the prosthetic connected, 'what's wrong?' Rachel asked as she saw Jana flinch.

'It's a little tender around the stump, can you look at it? I can't see the area that hurts.' Jana asked.

'Yes, of course' Rachel replied, she was nervous as she did not know what to expect she had never seen a stump before. Rachel did not show Jana her fears and standing behind Jana, she gasped as she saw how raw it was. Rachel explained to Jana what she could see, 'we had better get you to the hospital so they can look at it' Rachel said.

'No, that's not necessary, I can treat that myself. To be honest, I've neglected myself a bit where my arm is concerned, I've run out of lotion, and I need to get some bandages and new socks to put on my arm, I didn't expect to stay in Lanzarote for so long.' Jana said.

'Come on, I know where there is a good chemist. We can go there first, then we can go and get some lunch. You need food, you missed breakfast' Rachel said.

'Yes, that would be nice, as long as you don't mind walking with a one-armed woman' Jana replied.

'Don't be silly, of course, I don't' Rachel said with a smile.

|It was not long before they found the chemist, Jana was relieved to see that the pharmacist could speak perfect English, this made it much easier for her to explain what she needed. The lotion, socks and bandages were all packed neatly into a bag, Jana thanked the pharmacist for all her help, and they headed to look for somewhere to have lunch. Jana remembered the café she had gone to with Gloria. She asked Rachel if she would like to go to the café. 'of course, which way' Rachel replied. Jana pointed to the direction that they needed to go, as they walked, Rachel began to talk about the private detective again. 'I really do think you need to speak to this man; I don't think he is going to give up Jana, I truly don't' Rachel said with concern. Jana shrugged her shoulders; they had arrived at the café. Sitting down, Jana took her attention to the menu; she really did not want to talk about this man. 'Ah, Jana' Maria said, smiling as she bent down to kiss Jana on the cheek. Maria took the menu away saying' No, no, Maria's special for you' before scurrying off to the kitchen.

'That was full-on, do you know her?' Rachel asked.

'Yes, that's Gloria's mother Maria' Jana said.

'Who's Gloria?' Rachel asked puzzled. Jana began to laugh, she forgot how nosey Rachel could be.

Jana was about to explain when Rachels phone went off. It's Louise, Rachel mouthed silently to Jana, as Rachel chatted away to Louise, Jana took in the atmosphere of the café. The tables were scattered chaotically around the room, table clothes covering them, and little vases of single flowers sat next to the menus in the middle. The age of the building made it look a bit neglected, but this added to the quaint look of it, despite its aged look the café was spotlessly clean and tidy. 'I don't think she is listening, she's off to her fairyland again' Rachel said as she waved a hand in front of Jana's face to get her attention. Jana looked at her to find Rachel handing the phone over to her, 'Louise would like to talk to you' Rachel said impatiently.

Louise explained that she would be longer getting back as her uncle Georges funeral had been put on hold, some of his troop were living abroad, and they wanted to attend the funeral, 'he was very much loved by one and all' Louise said.

'That's nice of them to come from abroad for his funeral' Jana said

'Rachel tells me you have to come back to the UK, something about your arm Louise said.

'That's right I must get it serviced, next Tuesday.' Jana replied.

'Would you like to come to the funeral that's not till Friday, we can travel back to Lanzarote together after that' Louise said with hope in her voice.

'I would like that, yes, but I'm not sure if I will be coming back to Lanzarote next week' Jana said. They arranged to meet at the local bus depot to Louise on Thursday afternoon, 'you're more than welcome to stay with us' Louise said.

'Thank you, I will see you on Thursday then' Jana said before hanging up the phone.

The phone call ended as Maria came to the table with their food. 'Papas Arrugadas and Gofio, eat, eat' Maria said gesturing towards the meal.

'Thank you, Maria, it looks delicious' Jana said. Maria walked away to leave them to eat their meal in peace.

'What's this?' Rachel asked with a puzzled look.

'I'm not sure' Jana said as she broke off a piece of the Gofio.

The meal was spicy, they could taste, peppers, herbs and garlic, and there were also potatoes. The meal just as it looked was delicious and tasty. Jana began to laugh as she watched Rachel open her mouth and start to fan it with her hand. 'that's hot' Rachel said, breathing in and out rapidly as she tried to cool her mouth down. The meal finished they sat and had a coffee before paying for their lunch and leaving. 'Thank you, Maria, that really was a tasty meal.' Jana said.

After lunch they walked along the street, looking into the windows of the shops and chatting it was not long before they found themselves down by the sea. Finding a seat, they both sat quietly watching the world go by. Jana watched as a catamaran sailed by, 'would you like to go on one of them with me tomorrow,' she asked Rachel, pointing over to it.

'Why not, let's go and book a trip' Rachel replied eagerly, she had wanted to go on one for a while, but Stuart was not so keen. They looked around for one of the shops where they could book a trip on a catamaran. Soon they had the trip booked and headed back to the apartment.

'Whew, it is hot today,' Jana said, brushing her hand across her forehead.

'Why don't we go for a swim?' Rachel replied

'No, you go ahead I'll watch you' Jana replied as she looked towards her arm.

'Have you been swimming since you had the accident?' Rachel asked recalling that she had never seen Jana swimming.

'To be honest no, I never had the confidence after the accident.' Jana replied

'What would you tell one of your clients in your situation?' Rachel said in a slightly abrupt manner.

'Swimming would be an excellent exercise to strengthen the muscles' Jana replied honestly

Rachel was not letting go, she continued to push. 'Yes, but what about their self-esteem, what would you say about that?' Rachel asked. Jana knew what she was getting at and refused to respond. 'You know you will have to get over these things sooner or later Jana. Better for it to be sooner rather than later you know' Rachel said trying to encourage Jana to move forward with her life.

'Yes, I know. I can't go in the pool today, not with my arm like this. Jana said

'Mm, ok, but that won't stop you sitting on the edge of the pool, dangling your feet in to cool you off will it' Rachel replied smiling. Jana smiled back and shook her head in response. Jana knew that Rachel was right, she had been putting things off for some time now. Jana knew that it was the time that she sorted her life out once and for all, there could be no looking back. Jana had to look forward now. With determination in her mind, Jana promised herself that she would accept what had happened to her and not dwell on it. 'About time' a little voice in her head said.

The first thing Jana knew she had to do was to confront the private detective and find out what he wanted of her. *"That can wait for now,"* Jana thought. She stayed at the pool for a couple of hours taking in the sun's rays and cooling her feet in the water, intermittently chatting to Rachel. When she was fed up and had enough of the pool, Jana returned to the apartment and searched out the number for the detective. Nervously she waited as the call went through. Jana arranged to meet him in the reception area later that evening. As time went by, Jana became more nervous, she remembered what had happened the last time she met him. Jana had asked Rachel to be there for moral support. Rachel had replied that there 'no way' she would allow Jana to meet him alone. Rachel had said this with a determination in her tone of voice, she had reassured Jana that she would be safe with her there. As they sat and waited, they wondered what this man wanted of Jana.

As he entered the reception area, Rachel recognised the private detective and instantly stood up, as if to protect Jana from him. He shook Jana's hand as he introduced himself to her, he had seen Rachel standing up with determination to defend Jana and apologised to Jana for the accident. 'I am Richard Wilson, and I am a private detective. I am so, so sorry; I did not mean to scare you the last time we met' he said as he continued to shake Jana's hand. Jana, determined not to let her fear show, replied adamantly. 'What I would like to know is why you have you have been searching for me and why you did not approach me that day in the marketplace? You have been following me for some time, you have had me scared the whole time and not just the last time we met.' The private detective attempted to apologise again, but Jana was having none of it.

Jana wanted a full explanation, a rationale as to why he would feel it necessary to creep around following women. 'Let's start with the day at the market, shall we' Jana said. She could feel all the anger coming to the boil and needed to hear what he had to say. 'I agree it's the least you owe her' Rachel said as she could feel Jana's anger. Stuart feeling the tension in the air asked them all to go to the lounge area for a coffee, he was secretly hoping this would help to calm Jana down. Rachel took the lead, giving Jana time to calm down. 'Mr Wilson, would you start at the beginning please and tell us who has hired you and why?' Rachel asked the question, knowing it was what Jana would have asked. 'Yes certainly, but please call me Richard' he said as he looked at Jana. 'I was hired by Callum's brother, he hired me to look for the woman who saved his brother's life, he wants the opportunity to thank you for himself.' he said again directing it all to Jana.

Jana persisted with the questions, she wanted to know everything. 'What makes you possibly think that this woman is me?' Jana asked naturally, still seething.

'Because the young man Callum, had a friend with him called Chris' as he spoke of Chris, he looked for signs in Jana to see if there was any recognition.

'What did this Chris say' Jana asked.

'Chris gave a precise description of the woman and of her difficulty when helping Callum,' Richard was looking at her arm. 'That day in the market, I sat next to you to see if your arm was false. It is so realistic that I could not see it from a distance. I did not mean to scare you; I can only apologise again for that' he said as he continued.

'You could have asked me, and not just sat and stared at me' Jana was relaxing a little, this man did not appear to be anyone she should fear, 'he's just someone doing his job,' she thought. 'Please continue' Jana said not giving him a chance to answer.

'Callum's brother would like to meet you personally so that he can thank you' Richard continued.

Rachel interrupted the conversation and began asking questions. Richard's face showed that he was not pleased by the interruption, Rachel did not care and proceeded with her own questions

'Why??' Rachel said.

'Actually, both he and Chris would like to meet you properly' Richard said, ignoring Rachel's question.

'That won't be necessary, I don't need to be thanked for helping someone, I am just glad he is alright.' Jana said. Rachel looked at Jana, she could not believe what she was hearing, she had been suspicious that Jana had been the young lady but had not been sure until now. The air was becoming tense again, and so Rachel tried to make light of things, 'Stuart told me the lady couldn't just disappear' she said

'On the contrary, that is exactly what happened, it took me a while to find you. Are you sure you will not meet up with Callum's brother?' Richard said.

'No, as I said, there is no need for them to thank me. Now if that is all Mr Wilson? I have things to do' Jana spoke in a manner that warned him not to proceed.

He stood, and as he shook her hand, thanked her for her time. Jana, however, knew that this would not be the last time that she would see Richard Wilson, they watched as he walked out of the hotel. When he was out of earshot, Rachel asked Jana why she could not meet Cullum's brother and more importantly, why she had not told her that it was her on the beach rescuing Callum that day. Jana just merely shrugged her shoulders and said, 'I was just able to help, I didn't do it on my own.'

The subject was dropped, and Jana decided to go for a walk. 'I'll come with you' Rachel said.

'I'll be alright, I am feeling much better now. I will see you when I get back. Jana said firmly. Jana had taken this walk numerous times over the past few weeks and felt well enough to go alone. As she walked Jana's thoughts went to her future, Jana knew that she needed to go back home to sort out her life and decided that it would be the opportunity to do so next week when she went back to Britain for her hospital appointment. Walking along, she passed one of the quaint little shops that would be missed when she went home. Jana decided to call in and purchase a notebook and pad. Jana felt it was about time she had more structure in her life. The first thing was to make a list of her needs and wants and then decide in what direction her life would take. Jana smiled to herself as she realised that she was now looking forward to her future.

She continued to walk until she found herself by the beach, Jana sat on the stone bench that she had occupied many times since coming to the island. Jana looked out onto the ocean, she was beginning to relax and enjoy the peace and quiet. This did not last long as Jana's peacefulness was broken by the sound of a little girl laughing. Jana smiled as she watched the little girl laughing. Her smile fading when she realised that the little girl was in a wheelchair. 'Oh daddy, I will be alright here, you must go to the toilet before you wet yourself.' The little girl was hysterical now as she watched her father crossing his legs and rocking on the spot. She was holding her stomach as the laughter began to make it ache. Jana walked over to them. 'Would you like me to sit with your daughter while you find a toilet?' Jana asked.

The man looked at his daughter, his brows creasing together in desperation. 'Go on daddy, I will be fine with the lady she has a kind face' the little girl said as she looked at Jana. He looked at Jana and back to his daughter, but the pressure was too much, and he scurried off to the toilet. 'I'm Charlotte, but daddy likes to call me Charlie and my daddy's name is Brandon,' she said, smiling at Jana.

'Hi Charlotte, I'm Jana. She replied.

'What happened to your arm?' Charlotte asked. Jana had forgotten that she did not have her prosthetic arm on and that Charlotte could only see the bandaged stump. She did not have the time to answer Charlotte as her father arrived back. 'Thank you so much, I thought I was going to have to leave a puddle on the walkway.' he said, and the little girl began to laugh again.

'You're welcome.' Jana said, smiling as she waved goodbye to them both. Jana sat back on the bench she had vacated to help them; she had not been there long when she saw the ball of light again. She had become accustomed to the orb; she knew it was her angel. Sometimes the angel would show itself and at others would just merely float around like a ball of light. Jana knew that this time, it would not remain an orb as she could see it changing shape.

Her angel stood there beside her as she looked out onto the sea, 'you can speak with your mind, I will hear and understand you' the angel said to Jana. She realised that the angel had read her thoughts. She had thought that *"People around her would think she was insane"* as she spoke to herself. Smiling; Jana thanked her angel and asked why she had come to her. 'sometimes Jana you need to realise that with the smallest of things, you have changed someone's life' the angel said.

'What do you mean?' Jana asked puzzled.

'Just by simply sitting with that little girl, you have helped her to move down a new path in life.'

'I don't understand' Jana said

'You will when the time is right' the angel replied before vanishing.

'Why so, cryptic?' Jana shouted out to the angel aloud, then laughed to herself as she realised, she had said the words and people had begun to look at her. Yet no answer came from her angel. It was time to go back to the apartment,

Jana knew that Rachel would be worrying. She took her time going back, mentally making a list of what she would do to change her life. *"I'll have to put pen to paper tomorrow to make my list before I start my packing,"* Jana thought to herself, all she needed to do was to tell Rachel of her plans. Jana had a feeling that Rachel would not be too happy about it.

Rachel was watching a film when Jana returned to the apartment. She was smiling as she told her that Stuart would be returning on a flight the next day. Rachel had been eager to speak to Stuart about the baby and wanted to see for herself the look in his eyes. She knew Stuart well and knew that he would be worrying about having genetic tests done as much as she would. She discussed this with Jana hoping that Jana would be able to tell her everything would be alright. 'You will have to learn to relax Rachel, any undue stress will not be good for either you or the baby, take one day at a time.' Jana tried to advise her the best way that she could, she was not a midwife and could not answer the questions that Rachel was asking her. Jana thought better than to tell her about her own plans, *"It would be best left until Stuart arrived."* she thought to herself. 'What about going out for a meal and a show tonight?' Jana asked Rachel as she tried to take her mind off things.

'That sounds good, have you anything in mind?' Rachel asked.

'There is a club on the beachfront we could go and see who they have performing' Jana replied.

'That sounds good' Rachel said

'Right, I am going to have a lie-down, I can feel a headache coming on, I don't want it to spoil our night out on the town' Jana said as she got up to go into her room.

Rachel pottered around and tidied up as quietly as she could while Jana had a rest, once finished she went on to the veranda and settled in the shade with a refreshing drink to read her book. She thought she could hear Jana moving around in her room, but it was not until Jana screamed that she went in. Rachel watched as Jana began moving about on her bed, Rachel tried to wake her, but Jana continued to cry out and move around. Rachel didn't know what to do, she had never seen Jana like this, and it worried her. Jana was unaware that Rachel was even in the room, the man with no face had her by the arms, shaking her, he was shouting 'where is it, where is the stuff?'

'I don't know, I don't know what you are talking about.' Jana kept telling him. The more she said she did not know, the harder he began to shake her.

Rachel was getting concerned and tried to wake Jana again, 'Jana what don't you know?' She said. Jana woke suddenly, and when she saw Rachel, she sobbed bitterly into her shoulder.

'Jana, you have to tell me what these dreams are about? Rachel said.

'I wish I could explain what they are about, I just don't know. All I know is that the dream repeats itself and each time it reveals a little more' Jana said sobbing.

'My God Jana, you should see yourself thrashing around the bed, you gave me a scare' said Rachel quite bluntly. Jana tried to explain about the men in the dream and how they are kidnapping another man, she told her of the man with no face and how he kept grabbing her, but this time he was looking for something from Jana. Jana could not explain to Rachel what it was as she did not know herself.

Rachel made Jana a cup of sweet herbal tea to help Jana calm down. 'Have you seen anyone? a doctor maybe about these dreams' Rachel asked.

'No, I don't know what anyone could do about them' Jana replied.

'They might be able to help you to define what they mean and where they fit into your own life, it's obvious your worried about something' Rachel said

'I'll think about seeing someone' Jana promised, she had seen enough doctors but knew that she would need to see one as the dreams were getting worse. 'Anyway, it's time to get ready to go to that show, I'm going to take a shower' Jana said, trying to change the subject. They were both ready to leave for the town when the phone rang, it was Louise. Rachel answered the phone. 'Hi Rachel, I just wanted to catch up with you. I miss you both so much.' said Louise

'it's Louise,' Rachel said, turning to Jana. Rachel told her all about the message that Jana had given her and how precise Jana had been. Jana could hear Louise screaming congratulations from across the room, as she took in the news about the baby.

Rachel handed Jana the phone, and she chatted for a short while with Louise before hanging up and heading out through the door, Rachel had gone down to reception already, and Jana met her there. On arriving at the reception, Jana could see that Rachel was not alone. Richard Wilson, the private detective, was with her. 'What do you want?' Jana asked.

'I've come to try and persuade you to meet with Callum's brother, he is on the island of Lanzarote as we speak' he said. The detective had been trying to convince Rachel to help persuade Jana to meet him, Rachel had in no uncertain terms told him where to go. 'I have told you; I have no intentions of meeting that man, now or ever, please leave me alone Mr Wilson' Jana said

'I would, but he is not happy that you won't see him so that he can thank you personally.' He said.

'Well, that is his problem, if he can't accept that I won't meet up with him' Jana replied. Jana gave the detective such a stare that Rachel thought she was going to throw a punch at him.

Chapter Five:
In the Presence of Angels

Jana was getting angry, *'Who does this man think he is?* Jana thought. He can't demand that people meet with him, you just tell him to leave me alone' Jana said as she turned on her heels to go, leaving Rachel practically running to catch her, the private detective stared at the back of Jana in dismay. The detective knew that his employer would not like to be told to leave her alone. Picking up his phone, he relayed the message from Jana to his employer, he could hear him sigh on the other side of the phone. He was a man that was not accustomed to being told no. The one thing Callum's brother had done, even if he could not get to meet Jana was to get Rachel's curiosity running away with her. 'I wonder what he looks like' Rachel said.

'Who?' asked Jana.

'You know Callum's brother' Rachel said.

'I expect he is a bossy old man' Jana said. Rachel began to laugh, and they continued their walk. They walked along in silence, looking for the clubs and restaurants to see what entertainment was available when Rachel lifted her hand up to her chest and sighed.

'What's wrong?' Jana asked.

'Look at that poor child over there' Rachel replied and pointed to someone in a wheelchair.

Jana recognised the chair she had noticed the bright pinkness of it when she had met Charlotte earlier that day. 'Come on' she said to Rachel. Rachel had a job to keep up with Jana walking speedily. *"What's she doing now"* Rachel thought to herself.

'Hi Charlotte' Jana said to the little girl in the chair.

'Hi Jana' Charlotte answered her smiling.

'This is my friend Rachel, where's your father?' Jana said as she introduced Rachel to Charlotte.

'He's just there getting me an ice cream cone' Charlotte said pointing to the ice cream vendor.

'Would you and your friend like one' Charlotte's father was shouting.

'No thank you' Jana shouted back shaking her head.

'Charlotte, I hope you're nice to the ladies, she has a mean streak' her father said when he returned with his daughter's ice-cream, looking directly at Jana as he said it.

'haven't we all' Rachel said laughing.

'Daddy I told you I like Jana; she has a kind face' Charlotte replied with a cheekiness about her.

'Thank you, Charlotte, I like you too' Jana said as she ruffled her hair.

'We had better go, or we will miss the show, bye Charlotte, nice to meet you' Rachel said

'Bye' Charlotte said waving to them.

'Bye and again thank you, Jana, for watching Charlotte this afternoon' Charlottes father said.

Rachel could not resist teasing Jana. 'He's dishy, who is he?' Rachel asked being nosy again. Jana told her about his dilemma this afternoon and how it had been evident that he didn't want to leave his daughter with a stranger. But that nature's call would not allow otherwise. Rachels curiosity satisfied, they found a venue with both good food and entertainment. It was a warm evening, and so they opted to eat outside looking out to sea. As they chatted, Jana kept thinking about Charlotte and her father, he was indeed a good-looking man who could make a woman's heart skip a beat. Jana had noticed his broad, muscular shoulders and his square Jaw. At six feet six inches, he was a tall man; Jana had measured many during her working career and seemed to have near-perfect ability to guess height and weight. Shaking her thoughts away, Jana felt a little disturbed by them, she had not thought of a man in this way since she had been with Justin. It was an effort to listen to the entertainment and what Rachel was saying when she chatted, Jana was finding it challenging to put Charlotte's father out of her mind.

As the night moved on, Jana was finding it more difficult and was glad when they went back to the apartment. 'What was wrong with you tonight, Jana? You were all over the place' Rachel said.

'I'm sorry Rachel, I don't feel very well, I think I'll go to bed.' Jana had lied to Rachel something she was not comfortable with, but she knew that Rachel would just go on about Charlotte's father and as she was trying to forget him, she would rather not chat about him. 'Goodnight Rachel' Jana said as she headed to bed.

'Night Jana' Said Rachel.

Jana found it hard to settle down and waited for Rachel to go to bed before coming out. She got herself a glass of cold lemonade and went out to the veranda. Jana sat on the sunbed this time looking up at the moon, it was not long before she was sleeping on the sunbed. Jana began dreaming again, the dream was different. This time she was dreaming of Charlotte's father, and it was him holding her arms this time and not the faceless man. Charlotte's father held Jana in a gentle, sweet way. Jana dreamt that they were standing on the beach in the moonlight, the breeze blowing her hair across her face. Brushing the hair away from her face and smiling, he turned her to look at the sea. He began pointing to something on the horizon, and as he held her close, she could feel the heat of his body protruding through his clothes onto her own body. Jana felt her heartbeat rapidly into her chest. Brandon was about to tell her what he was pointing at on the horizon when he turned her towards him and held her face in his hands; he leaned in to kiss her. Jana waited patiently for the kiss, she wanted him to take her, to make love to her right there on the beach. Her heart was beating so loudly and fiercely in her chest that it jolted her awake.

Jana reprimanded herself and told herself that he would never be interested in a woman like her, besides she would be going back to the UK soon. Jana could not dismiss the feeling that she had when she dreamt of charlottes father. Jana took herself off to bed and slept soundly throughout the night. Jana woke with a smile on her face, she did not understand why she was smiling, but just knew she felt good. The sun shone up in the sky, and the birds were singing when Jana woke. She purposefully missed her breakfast and went for her usual walk on the beach, deep down inside Jana was hoping to bump into Charlotte and her father again. Jana found herself smiling, everything seemed brighter and more colourful, the smell of the sea was uplifting, and the scent from the flowers planted along the seafront was being carried along in the air. Jana felt so happy inside, she felt like she was floating on air.

Running across the beach and kicking off her sandals, she ran into the refreshing sea giggling to herself. Realising that she was making a show of herself, she bit her lower lip and tried to refrain from dancing around like a schoolgirl. After all, *"Charlotte's father would not be thinking of her in the same way,"* Jana thought to herself. Jana's mood lowered a little after this, but she continued to paddle in the sea, still smiling, trying to keep her hopes up. She had not felt this good in a long time, *"I don't think I ever felt like this"* she thought. Reproaching herself, she thought, *"How can you think of a man you don't know like this; you have only met him on a couple of times."* Jana tried to put charlottes father to the back of her mind. She found a spot on the sand to sit on as she watched the people walk by. Jana saw a young couple and how happy they were smiling, laughing and running along the sand chasing each other. She longed to be loved in the same way. Shaking her head and brushing her hand through her hair, Jana decided that there was a need to forget looking for love and to start getting on with her life instead. She agreed with herself that it was the time she took a swim in the hotel pool. Jana had been both physically and mentally scarred following her accident, it was time she tackled the scars head on and defeat them in her own way.

Back at the apartment, Jana changed into her swimwear, she had chosen a black one-piece swimming costume, there were no frills about this get-up, Jana did not want to attract attention from anyone. Grabbing her towel, sun cream and a book she headed for the pool. She found a sun lounger in a sunny spot away from others. Jana had left her prosthetic hand behind and as usual, covered her arm from prying eyes. As she lay on the sunbed, she could feel the sun getting hotter on her skin, she reached for the lotion and began covering her legs and arms. Jana had in the past found it difficult to put cream on her right arm and shoulder because of the stump; determined she thought hard at how she could do this independently. Jana squeezed a significant amount of cream onto her thigh and dipped her stump in it, Jana then attempted to stretch her arm around as far as possible covering her arm and shoulder. Jana silently applauded herself, 'way to go girl' she thought with the task completed to the best of her ability.

As Jana looked up, she could see people looking at her, 'now is the time girl, don't worry about them, you have nothing to be ashamed of,' she told herself firmly. Jana looked across the pool and smiled at the people staring at her. She was laughing even harder to herself when she observed them becoming embarrassed, she picked her book up and continued to read. The book fell onto her chest as Jana nodded off in the heat of the sun, unsure how long she had been sleeping Jana woke with a start hearing her name being called 'Miss Heart.' It was the private detective, he was holding out a glass of water, realising that she was thirsty Jana took it off him.

'Thank you' Jana said

'I took the liberty of having ice put in the water, for you, it really is hot today.

'Yes, it is.

'You really should be careful, Miss Heart; you could get heatstroke sleeping in the sun like that.'

The detective was beginning to grind every nerve in Jana's body. 'What is it you want, Mr Wilson' Jana said as she could feel her anger rise to the surface. Does this man never give up, Jana thought to herself?

'Please call me Richard, I am afraid that my employer is not accepting that you won't meet with him.'

'That is my choice, Mr Wilson, and frankly, I don't care what that man thinks.' Jana refused to call him by his Christian name.

'All he wants to do is thank you in person for saving his brother's life.'

'As I told you before, there are no thanks needed, please go and tell him that.'

'I have tried many times, I'm sorry he is determined to meet with you soon.'

Jana was just about to tell them that she would be leaving the island soon but thought better of it. She would soon be back in the UK, and he wouldn't find her there. Jana excused herself and walked to the edge of the pool, looking back at the detective Jana smiled and said 'goodbye Mr Wilson' before diving in. Jana came to the surface of the water realising that she had not been swimming for a long time, let alone diving into one.

Another successful achievement, she reached over with her right hand a tapped herself on the back, smiling. 'What are you so happy about' a voice from the side of the pool said. Looking up, Jana could see it was Rachel. 'Today, I have decided to take the fate of my life into my own hands, well, so to speak, she said, shaking her stump toward Rachel. They both burst out laughing at the innocent way that Jana had responded. It felt nice to be able to laugh about it, Jana had cried too many times over losing her arm and hand, and it had been a massive effort on her part to get used to not having the use of her hand.

Over time Jana had to learn to live without the use of her arm and hand and had to adjust her way of thinking to be able to fulfil tasks without the use of them both. It was only now that Jana was coming to realise how well she had managed and that she had not given herself enough credit. 'Hold on I'm coming in' Rachel shouted as she slowly climbed into the pool and swam over to Jana. 'Well done, it's nice to see you swimming, what did the detective want?' Rachel's praise was short-lived, it was plain to see her nosy nerves were twitching for the answer. 'Oh, you are nosy,' Jana said before explaining why he had been there.

'Will he never give up?' Rachel asked

'I hope so, it's getting quite annoying' Jana replied.

'Maybe you would be better off meeting with Cullum's brother, he may leave you alone then.' Rachel said.

'No, I will not be dictated to by Callum's brother or anyone else' Jana said.

Changing the subject, 'I have some news for you. Stuart has made me an appointment to have the baby checked' Rachel said, smiling. Jana could see Rachel's smile stretching from ear to ear.

'That is good news, when is the appointment?' Jana asked.

'Ah, that's just it, it's the day after tomorrow, so we have to leave on the early morning flight tomorrow' Rachel Said.

'I have an appointment myself soon, so I will be leaving for the UK in a few days' Jana said.

'Please stay at our apartment, I will be back in a few weeks when I know the results of any test done for the baby' Rachel said.

'Thank you, we must make sure we keep in touch' Jana said hugging Rachel. They came out of the pool and sat on the side, swinging their legs in the water, staring into space until Rachels' stomach started to rumble. 'Time for a sandwich I think, would you like one?' Rachel said.

'Yes, please' Jana said

'You get the drinks, while I go and make them, ham and tomato?' Rachel asked as she got up to leave.

'That sounds nice,' Jana replied as she got up to go to the pool bar for their drinks.

Jana was back to reading her book. Rachel arrived back quicker than she expected with the sandwiches, 'What is the book about?' she asked

'Angels and their meanings, I thought I had better learn more about them, as they are a part of my life now.' Jana said, holding the book up for Rachel to read.

'That is so strange, how have you started to see angels at your age? Rachel asked not really knowing what she was talking about.'

'Well actually, I have only recently realised that the angels have been in my life since I was a child' Jana replied. Jana went on to tell Rachel about the dream where she had been able to see herself with her grandparents and how she had seen her angel standing over her, watching and protecting her. 'I had always felt something around me for a long time before that. I would wander off into my own little world, I just never knew what it was, the adults, of course, put it down to me having an imaginative friend, I now know it was my parents, and my angels' Jana said.

As they ate their sandwiches, Rachel continued to ask about the angels and asked if she and her unborn child had angels around them. Jana explained that her friend Gloria had told her that we all have guardian angels with us the moment that we are conceived. Rachel smiled as she stroked her stomach as if giving comfort to the unborn child within. The conversation was disrupted as one of the hotel staff approached Jana to tell her that there was a telephone call in reception for her.

'did they say who they were?' said Jana

'I'm sorry all I know it is a man' he said.

'I'll get that' Rachel said getting up to answer the call. Jana sat there eagerly waiting for Rachel to return. Jana could see that Rachel was not happy just by looking at the expression on her face. 'What an arrogant, rude man he is' Rachel said as she continued to tell Jana what had happened. 'Well, I tried to tell him that you did not want to see him and that you feel there is no need for a thank you, he started to get shirty and raise his voice at me.

Rachel explained the conversation in depth to Jana. 'The arrogance of the man he said that he wanted to talk to you and that I was not good enough. Oh, don't worry, I gave him a piece of my mind I can tell you' Rachel told Jana, it was apparent that she was furious. Jana smiled to herself; she could imagine how Rachel had reacted. 'He can be as arrogant as he wants, I am not going to see him, and he is just going to have to live with that.' Jana said.

'Ok, that's good, let's go and change, I fancy going out for a bit, would you like to join me.? Rachel asked, and Jana nodded in reply. Picking their things up, they headed back to the apartment to shower and change for their walk. They decided to go to the more traditional village, they had been told about a church there and how miracles happen to people when they visit there.

Rachel wanted to give the baby as much chance as possible, even though deep down, she was not religious. They had been told to make sure they visit the church at sunset, so that that they could see the beauty of the stained-glass windows themselves. It was a short bus journey to the village; the bus drove down the coast roads. Jana found the views to be gentle and relaxing, the evening sun shining on the sea, the sands running around the island like a dividing line between the sea and land. The sky was blue and clear of clouds. The occasional villa scattered around the area. Rachel had dozed off, her head resting on Jana's shoulder, when they arrived at the village, Jana gently nudged Rachel awake.

'We have arrived, it looks so beautiful' Jana said

'What, sorry Jana, I seem to be tired all the time.' Rachel said yawning.

'Thanks, ok, come on let's get off the bus Jana said.

'Whew, feel that heat' Rachel said as they got off the bus. They had not realised it was still so warm. They found somewhere where they could have a sweet cold drink.

They sat outside with their drink and took in the ambience of the village, there was no one rushing around, people were walking around leisurely and carefree around the town. Everyone was calm and relaxed; the politeness of the locals was evident in the way they said hello to them. The atmosphere of the area seemed different, it felt mystical and peaceful. They did not speak to each other as they drank their drinks and took it all in. The drinks finished they got up to explore the village a little more and to find the church they had been told about. 'There is something about this place, I don't know what it is, but I know I can feel something or is it that I can feel nothing.' Rachel said.

'I know what you mean, I agree I think it's more nothing than something.' Jana replied. They went on to say how they could feel no anger, no anxiety, no frustration, no worry or concern. 'How is this possible?' Rachel asked. Jana just shrugged her shoulders, they continued to walk the streets until they found the little church.

When they entered the church, the atmosphere likened to the one in the village, except it felt more profound more mystifying. They each moved to the opposite side of the church to look at the structure of the marble figures and religious artefacts and pictures that hung on the wall, reading each inscription on them. They smiled as they passed each other to complete the same process on the opposite side. They met where they started at the entrance to the church, catching each other's hands, nervously they walked down the centre of the church toward the altar. The sun was going down, and they could see the rays coming through the stained-glass windows above the altar. Their breath was taken away as they stood in awe, looking up at the windows. Jana could see thousands of balls of lights in the sun's rays, while Rachel saw blue light flowing from the sun's rays.

As the sun lowered in the sky, the lights moved closer to Jana and Rachel, they were experiencing different things but were unaware of it. As the lights moved closer, Jana found herself in the presence of angels, their wings spreading out widely gently enveloping her. The feeling was so intense, it was unexplainable, she felt all her own anxieties and fears lifting. Jana saw her own guardian angel standing at the side of the altar smiling at her and looking on as the angels immersed her. Jana looked over at Rachel, she had a look of shock on her face, tears were running down her cheeks as she stared up into the light. Looking around the church, the marble statues appeared to come to life, it was as if they were watching them. She looked back at the angels, the auras around each individual one was a different and vibrant colour, their enormous wings were spread out wide.

Jana could feel the love coming from each one, she looked at her angel and the angels of the light and thanked them for the love and protection that they were giving her. Smiling the angels started to rise back to the heavens, and the sun rays began to move away. Jana could feel her tears running down her cheeks, she knew now that the feeling of love she had from her own angel was but a mere fraction of what she felt at that moment. Jana's angel nodded towards her and smiled before disappearing. Rachel turned towards Jana, 'did you see it? did you see the light?' Jana realised that Rachel had experienced something different. Jana worried that it might be too much for Rachel, she suggested they go for a meal where they could discuss what had happened. As they left the church, they lit the candles of remembrance in memory of loved ones who had passed. Rachel slipped her arm into Jana's and almost skipped out of the church, they found a local restaurant, 'Come on, let's go in and eat' Jana said.

Their meal and some cold orange juices ordered; they began to talk about what had happened in the church. Rachel was eager to tell Jana about the blue light. 'I just can't explain the feeling Jana, I want to be able to explain it to you, I just don't know how.' Jana smiled, 'I think I know how you feel, and I certainly know how hard it is to explain it to others. Why don't you start with what you saw, that may explain some of the feelings you experienced' Jana suggested.

'Ok, where do I start is the problem. When we entered the church, I felt drawn to the architecture and artefacts, I've never been interested in that sort of thing, I just couldn't help myself. I never even noticed that we were not together until we met back at the entrance. Oh, Jana the feeling I had was exceptional, then when we held hands and walked down to the altar and the light came in through the windows, and the blue coming from the light was so vivid, so clear.'

Rachel continued with excitement on her face, 'then I was surrounded by the blue light, it felt warm and safe. There was a feeling inside of me, a tingling, it was vibrating through me, through my veins. Jana, it felt so good, I could feel it inside me inside my heart, it flowed down into my womb. Oh, I wish I could explain it properly to you.' The tears were running down Rachels' face again as she was explaining what had happened. Rachel reached over and squeezed Jana's hand. 'Now, it's your turn to tell me what happened to you, Jana.' Rachel said excitingly.

'I had the same experience, the same feeling as you until we stood before the altar.' Jana went on to explain to Rachel about the angels their auras and their wings, the feelings she had received from them. 'I find it challenging to describe them as well, but you know I don't think that anyone will experience the same things, we are all individuals and have different needs, I feel that we each only experience what we need to Jana said.

Rachel nodded in response, she understood precisely what Jana meant. They ate their meal in silence and decided to get a taxi back to the apartment, Rachel was going home tomorrow and needed to get some rest before the long flight. 'I don't think I will be able to sleep tonight after that' Rachel said to Jana as they rode in the taxi back.

'I'm sure you will, we both will.' Jana replied. The taxi dropped them off at the hotel entrance, back at the apartment, Jana made some tea for them both and took it out to the veranda where Rachel joined her.

Standing up and looking out over the sea, Jana took in a deep breath, 'I am going to miss you when you go home tomorrow' she said to Rachel.

'I'm going to miss you too, Rachel said with tears in her eyes.

'We will only be separated by miles of roads when we are back in the UK, but that won't stop me from coming to see you, Jana said.

'I hope so, I want you in our lives, I want you to be there when the new life is born' Rachel said, rubbing her stomach. Jana hugged Rachel and promised to be there with her when she had her baby. 'Now, time for bed you, you and the little one have a long journey ahead of you tomorrow' she said as she encouraged Rachel to get some sleep.

Rachel smiled and hugging Jana said, 'goodnight, my dear friend.'

'Goodnight dear lady, sweet dreams' Jana said.

After Rachel went to bed, Jana turned back towards the sea, taking in another deep breath, she would honestly miss Rachel and Louise's company, she missed them already. Jana had felt a connection with them both since the first day she had met each one. Jana sat on the veranda for a while before, picking up the dishes and taking them into the kitchen to clean up before going to bed herself. It was not long before she was sleeping, and the dream started again. Jana was back in the street, where they were, the same three men. One man fighting to get away from the other two without success. Jana did not feel scared in the dream, not this time. The man with no face began to chase her again, Jana stood still and looked directly at him. She was ready this time when he grabbed her arms. Jana was prepared to fight. The man with no face was shaking her vigorously, he looked over her shoulder and stopped, he turned and ran back to his car.

Jana turned in the direction he had been looking in, a man was running towards her, as he got nearer to her, she could see that it was Brandon, Charlotte's father. 'Are you ok? who was that?' he asked Jana.

'I don't know' Jana replied as he put his arms around her as if to protect her. Then he was gone. Jana had woken from the dream, she tried to go back to the vision but could not bring it back into her mind, and so she got up and made a coffee. Jana knew that she would not be able to go back to sleep after that and taking her coffee out into the fresh air she sat by the table on the veranda and watched as the sun came up in the sky.

The hours moved by without Jana realising, she had been lost in her own reflections, Rachel disrupted her thoughts when she brought out some breakfast. 'You look like you could do with this' Rachel said as she placed it on the table, Jana looked up at Rachel and smiled before getting up off the lounger she had been occupying to sit at the table. 'How did you sleep?' Rachel asked. Jana told her about the dream and the changes that it entailed, and how again she had been in Charlotte's father's arms, feeling safe and secure. 'You should really go and see someone about those dreams, it is no wonders your all over the place' Rachel said as she expressed her concerns about Jana. Jana shrugged her shoulders and smiled before changing the subject. Rachel looked at her thoughtfully, she knew deep down that Jana would not see anyone about the dreams, all Rachel could do was hope that Jana would see sense and go and see someone.

It was not long before Jana was waving goodbye to Rachel as she entered the departure lounge at the airport. As Jana hugged Rachel, she made her promise that she would let her know the outcomes of the test, 'of course I will, I promise' Rachel said. As she went through the doors. Rachel blew a kiss to Jana and shouted' keep safe, please'. Jana nodded and waved before turning on her heels, she did not want Rachel to see her crying. Feeling alone again, Jana had been feeling safe and secure with both Rachel and Louise, and now they were both gone. Jana started to feel homesick for her own home and decided that she would bring forward her flight. As Jana walked over to the travel kiosk, someone was calling her name, she turned to find that it was Charlotte, this time she was with a woman. 'Hi, Jana' Charlotte said with a big smile on her face.

'Hello sweetheart, are you ok' Jana said as she kneeled to be at the same level as Charlotte.

'No, Daddy has had to go back to the states, to sort out some business' Charlotte replied as the smile left her face.

'I'm sure he won't be long; he would not want to leave this beautiful face for long, would he?' Jana said as she held Charlotte's face in her hands. Charlotte blushed a little and smiled in response. 'This is Sandra, my nanny. I don't know why daddy thinks I need a nanny; I can look after myself' Charlotte gave a huge sigh as she introduced the nanny. Jana attempted to shake the nanny's hand to introduce herself. Sandra, however, had other ideas, come on Charley, it's time to go' she said as she spun Charlotte around in her wheelchair.

Jana could hear Charlotte shouting at Sandra 'Don't call me that, only daddy can call me that' Charlotte replied, Jana could listen to the hurt as she said it. It was evident that Charlotte did not feel comfortable with Sandra. 'I will call you want I want, you're a spoiled little madam, that's what you are a spoiled young lady.' Sandra said nastily to Charlotte, forgetting that she was within earshot of Jana.

'Wait' Jana shouted, rushing over to Charlotte, Jana placed a piece of paper in Charlotte's hand, as she leaned forward to whisper in her ear,' you call me on this number, and I will keep you company over the phone while daddy is away.' She winked at Charlotte and kissed her on the cheek, Charlotte nodded and smiled in response. Jana did not like the way the nanny spoke to Charlotte; she made a mental note to talk to Charlotte's father the next time she saw him.

Jana turned and headed back to the travel kiosk to find it closed. There stood in front of it was her angel. 'It is not the time to go back, you must stay a little longer' the angel told her. Jana looked around to see if anyone else could see her angel, no one could it seemed until Jana saw a small crying child in a pram, she watched as the angel leaned forward and wrapped its wings around the little boy. The little boy stopped crying, and Jana watched as he fell into a gentle sleep. Jana heard the mother talking to the child's father, 'at last, he has not slept for days properly since he picked up a stomach bug' she said with a sigh of relief. Jana could see that the child's mother looked worn out and felt sorry for her. She looked back at the angel who was smiling at her, as she said, 'there is another child that needs your help, Jana, you must stay on the island to help.' Jana knew the angel was right and smiling nodded in response. The angel was gone as quick as it had arrived.

Jana made another mental note, 'I need to find out my angels name' she thought to herself as she did so she could hear a faint chuckling in the distance, Jana knew this was spirit and chuckled to herself in response. Jana was shocked to see that the Kiosk was open again, but instead of changing her flight time, she cancelled it. *"Now for my accommodation while I'm here,"* she thought.

Jana decided to call Stuart and tell him that Rachel was on her flight and that it had taken off, before asking him for a big favour. 'Stuart, would it be possible for me to rent the apartment from you, I would like to stay in Lanzarote a bit longer if I can.'

'You can stay at the apartment, Jana, but there is no way we are going to take any rent from you' Stuart replied.

'I can't accept that Stuart, I have to pay my way' she said with stubbornness in her voice, Jana was not aware that Start could be stubborn as well.

'Right then if you want to stay at our apartment then you can pay by making sure that it is clean and tidy, I will let the manager know that you have full permission to organise any repairs. That is the only deal I will accept' Stuart said in a firm voice.

Jana knew she was beaten, 'thank you, Stuart, I appreciate it. Jana said as she gave in to his demands 'you are very welcome my dear friend' Stuart replied in a gentler tone

'Please remind Rachel to ring me when she arrives' Jana asked him

'I will, and it won't be long before we see you again' he said, he had heard the sadness in Jana's voice and did not feel comfortable with it.

Stuart contacted the manager of the apartment, they had been friends for some years, he asked if he could keep a close eye on Jana for them, once reassured that his request would be fulfilled, he was happy. Stuart knew that Rachel would worry about Jana and he could not allow the extra stress, not with the baby. He also knew that he would be worried about her as well, they had both become fond of Jana. After hanging up the phone to Stuart, Jana got a taxi back to the apartment, she unpacked her clothes before walking down to the seafront for some lunch. Jana worried for Charlotte, she was a young disabled child and very vulnerable. Jana did not know what to do next, and her worries for the child continued to escalate. Jana was at the end of the beach; she had walked the length of the beach without knowing. All Jana could do was hope that Charlotte would contact her.

Chapter Six:

The Persistent Mr Black

Jana sat at her usual place on the concrete bench looking out to sea. Jana was lost in her thoughts; she did not notice a man sit beside her. 'Hello,' Richard Wilson said. Jana was getting annoyed with him, he would pop up at the most unusual moments, and every time he managed to startle Jana one way or the other.

'What do you want now?' Jana asked frustratingly

'Mr Black is still persistent; he still wants to meet with you.' he replied

'How many times do I have to tell you I do not want to meet him. Now please leave me alone and tell Callum's brother to leave me alone also, before I report you both to the authorities' Jana said.

Jana was getting angry now, she could not allow this to happen she had bigger things to worry about. Why would they persist in pursuing her this way? Jana turned to the detective 'tell me, did you ever tell your boss that you put me in the hospital?

'Well...' Jana was adamant she was going to get an answer despite the frightened look on his face.

'No, he would fire me on the spot and not pay me what he owes already, he can be quite stubborn' Richard said.

'Surely, he can't be that bad, can he?' Jana asked

'Yes, I'm afraid he can' he replied. He would not elaborate any further, and despite numerous questions from Jana, he kept tight-lipped. Jana was becoming intrigued; how can a man be so fearful of another man. *"What is it this man does, to be able to control someone in this manner?"* Jana thought to herself. 'I shall leave you in peace, Mr Wilson. As I said let your boss know I am not interested in meeting him please' Jana said as she stood up to leave.

'Call me Richard, please' he shouted after her.

Jana walked back to the apartment in a daze, all she could think about was Charlotte. She needed to find a distraction and decided to take a swim in the pool. Jana checked her stump it had been healing well, she would be able to use her prosthetic arm again soon, this thought reminded her she would need to cancel her appointment until a later date and tell Louise.

'Hello.' Louise said as she answered the phone.

'Hi Louise, it's Jana. I am so sorry, I won't be able to attend the funeral.' Jana said with a tremble in her voice.

'Now, now. There is no need for that, you have gone through so much. Please don't worry' Louise said.

They chatted for a while about Rachel and the baby. Louise asked how Jana was coping with things. Jana told her about the private detective and how tedious she was finding his pursuit on behalf of his employer to thank her. Louise made her promise that she would not let him get her down. 'Promise me, Jana, you are sounding worn out. Please don't let him wear you down' Louise said.

'I won't, I promise' Jana said. She had more to worry about than this Mr Black.

'I have to tie up a few loose ends, and I have an appointment to finalise things with uncle George's solicitor. I should be back in Lanzarote in a week or two, will you still be there, I do hope so, I miss you so much my dear friend' Louise said hopefully.

'Yes, I will be, Rachel and Stuart have kindly let me stay at their apartment' Jana replied cheerfully.

'Good, I will see you soon.' Rachel said, reminding her that she was welcome to use her apartment.

Jana looked down at her phone and realised that she had missed some incoming calls, she prayed it was not Charlotte. She must have missed the phone calls when she was deep in thought or conversing with Richard Wilson. Jana checked the number to find it was Rachels number. Jana called Rachel and was pleased to hear from her. 'Where have you been, you have me worried, I've tried to call you a dozen times,' Rachel said in exaggeration.

'I am so sorry; I was at the beach' Jana said, not telling Rachel that she had the phone with her all the time she was there. Rachel told her what the gynaecologist had said.

'They are going to keep a close eye on the new life and myself, he tried to reassure me that because Catherine had the gene, it does not mean that this little one will have it as well' Rachel said. Jana could still hear the worry in Rachel's voice.

'I see you've stuck to the pet name of new life' Jana said chuckling

'Yes, I feel Catherine named it for a little while when she called it a new life. Rachel's tone sounded brighter.

They chatted about Louise and Jana told Rachel how Louise had said she would be coming back out to Lanzarote soon. 'Good, the gynaecologist told me I need to rest, and so I thought I would head back out myself, where better to relax than among my friends' Rachel said. They made plans to stay in touch until Rachel could come back to Lanzarote before they both said goodbye. Jana was beginning to ache all over, that swim was calling out to her aching body. She changed into her swimwear and headed to the pool, making sure she took her phone with her. Jana ordered a cold refreshing drink before going for a swim. She sat at the edge of the pool drinking and looked over to see a teenage girl staring at her.

Jana called the girl and asked her if everything was alright, and the teenager blushed, realising that Jana had caught her staring. 'I am so sorry; I did not mean to stare at you' she said apologising.

'That's ok, I'm used to people staring now. Would you like to talk about it?' Jana asked the teenager as she introduced herself. 'Hi, I'm Carly, I was just wondering how you would be coping with only one hand?' the teenager replied honestly.

They discussed how she managed and the excellent support that she had from friends, they swam together for a while, Carly watched every stroke in the water that Jana made and was disappointed when Jana's phone rang, Jana, excused herself, picking up her phone she headed back to the apartment. Jana was pleased to find that it was Charlotte on the phone and that she sounded a lot happier than she had done earlier in the day. Charlotte told Jana that her grandparents were visiting and that they had given Sandra her nanny the rest of the day off. Charlotte informed Jana that the nanny was nasty and not a nice person.

'Have you told your grandparents about her' Jana asked.

'Yes, but its daddy's decision to have her and there is nothing they can do about that' Charlotte replied.

'I'm sure if you talk to your father and let him know how the nanny treats you and how you feel about it, I'm sure he will get you a new nanny.' Jana said. They chatted a while longer before Jana could hear a woman's gentle voice calling Charlotte.

'Bye Jana, I have to go granny is calling me, can I call you again please' Charlotte asked.

'Of course, you can' Jana replied before Charlotte hung up the phone.

Jana began to feel hungry; she was feeling better now that she had heard the happiness in Charlotte's voice. She showered and got herself ready to go for a meal and to watch some of the entertainment that was on offer that night. Jana had seen the poster on the way into the reception area earlier that day, there was going to be a band and a hypnotist. Jana wished she had company but promised herself she would try and enjoy it the best she could. Choosing a light fish supper, Jana called over the waiter and placed her order along with a bottle of wine, she had finished taking the medications prescribed by the doctor at the hospital and looked forward to having a drink again. There was calming music playing in the background, and Jana sat back and listened, taking in every gentle note. She shut her eyes as she listened to the music, her thoughts wandering off, she found herself thinking about Brandon. The waiter came with her wine and reassuring her that her meal would not be much longer offered further assistance to pour the wine. Jana declined the offer and thanked the waiter.

Pouring herself a glass of wine, Jana continued to listen to the music and found herself humming to the tune and realised that she had been smiling as she did so. Her meal was being placed in front of her, and it looked delicious. Jana felt self-conscious as she ate her food, she had not been alone since before she met Rachel, and now found herself longing for company. Looking around, she discovered that there were mostly couples in the restaurant with only a few families, she was the only one alone. As Jana finished her meal, her phone rang, not recognising the number, Jana thought better of answering the telephone. She left a tip on the table for the waiter and thanked him for his service, before leaving the restaurant and finding a pleasant spot to watch the entertainment.

While she waited for the entertainment to begin her phone began to ring again it was the same number, Jana decided to answer it, it's probably a cold caller she thought to herself. Cautiously Jana answered the phone, 'hello'.

'Hello, is that Jana?' a male voice enquired

'Yes, it is, who's calling please' Jana asked not recognising the voice on the other end of the phone.

'It's Brandon, Charlotte's father. I am sorry to bother you.'

'Is Charlotte alright?' Jana interrupted him mid-sentence.

'Well, it's Charlotte I'm calling about.'

'Charlotte has been telling me that you told her to talk to me about Sandra, her nanny.'

'Yes, that's right, I saw Charlotte and her nanny at the airport. The nanny was quite rude to Charlotte, and she upset her, so I told Charlotte to tell you about her' Jana explained.

'Yes, it seems that you are not the only one to have concerns about the nanny with Charlotte, her grandparents have also expressed their concerns. Up until now, I thought they were just overprotective of Charlotte, but it appears that I have been wrong.' Brandon said.

Brandon went quiet for a while before speaking again 'Jana I have something to ask you, I would not ordinarily do this; however, Charlotte insists that I talk to you and ask you.' 'Unfortunately, I can't let the nanny go just because she was rude to Charlotte. Again, the phone went quiet as he paused the conversation. Until I can investigate the nanny situation further, I was wondering if you would sit with Charlotte for a couple of days until I return. I would not ask you to give up your time like this, but Charlotte is adamant that she wants you to watch her and no one else while I am away, I'll pay you for watching her of course.' He said 'Of course, I will, I quite like Charlottes company.' Jana replied. Brandon thanked her and said that he would send a car to pick her up at ten o'clock the following morning.

Jana went back to watching the show. The hypnotist had a man on stage who believed he was a woman, he was wearing a woman's bra over his clothing and was attempting to do the bra up, people roared with laughter as he went around and around trying to complete the task. Next to the man on stage was a woman who believed she was a man, she began stomping around as if wearing big boots, she walked over to the man and taking the bra strap out of his hands said 'come here woman, you'd swear you never did this before.' The crowd laughed even louder, and Jana found herself laughing just as loud. Deep inside, she wondered if it was because of the show or because she now knew she would get to see Brandon and Charlotte again. For the rest of the show, Jana's thought was distracted with the excitement of seeing Brandon again. The remainder of the show ended with Jana only catching glimpses of it. Jana returned to the apartment after the show and made herself a coffee and went to sit on the veranda.

It was a lovely night; the moon was shining as she lay on the lounger and listened to the waves crashing onto the shore. Jana loved the sound of the waves it always helped her to relax, there was a distant rumble of thunder, she looked out across the sea and saw sheets of lightning across the sky far away into the distance. The roll of thunder grew louder, she began to count one, two, three silently to herself. Jana remembered the old saying her grandmother used to tell her if you can count in between the thunderclaps and lightning strikes then that's how many miles away the storm is. Jana continued to listen out for the thunder and watched for the lightning until she could feel raindrops hitting her. Jana went inside and sat with the veranda windows open, storms interested her and found them to be invigorating. Watching the rain until she felt sleepy, she silently thanked the angel and then went to bed, Jana slept deeply throughout the night.

Jana woke to the sun shining and the birds singing, she had not slept so well in years. She was looking forward to looking after Charlotte and was disappointed to find it was only seven o'clock in the morning. She took herself off to the beach, she always liked to see what the sea had thrown up onto the beach following a storm. Looking around, Jana found a large piece of green sea glass, it shimmered in the sunlight. She placed the glass into her pocket before searching for more, this time she saw a red bit of sea glass in the shape of a heart. As Jana picked it up, hearing a female voice whisper in her ear, for Charlotte with all my love. Jana knew in her heart that this was the voice of Charlotte's mother and decided that she would have it made into a necklace. Checking the time, Jana thought it was time to go back, Jana needed to be ready for the car

Brandon was sending for her. Jana had already packed her things up, now all she needed to do was let her friends know her plans.

Picking up her phone, she called Rachel; first, Rachel was pleased and excited for her. She wished Jana well and made her promise that she would tell her every detail of her stay with Brandon and Charlotte. Now it was Louise's turn, Jana had expected Louise to respond differently, and indeed Louise did. She was full of concerns, telling Jana that she did not know Brandon. Louise made Jana promise to be careful and to keep in contact with her, expecting at least two phone calls a week from Jana. As she hung up her mobile call, the apartment phone was ringing. The hotel staff were ringing the apartment to tell Jana that her car had arrived, Jana went outside to look for the taxicab. Having not found her ride outside, she went back to the reception desk, the woman behind the counter looked at her with confusion and took her out to the car herself.

The only car outside was a limousine, the staff member went to speak to the driver and then beckoned Jana over, 'this is your car miss she told Jana. Jana looked stunned as the chauffeur took her bags and placed them in the boot of the car before opening the door for her. Jana slipped into the limousine and felt the leather seating under her hands as she did so. Jana in shock, feeling excited but at the same time was confused, why had such a car been sent, Jana had never been in a limousine before. There was nothing Jana could do until arriving at Charlotte's house, she planned on speaking to her father about it. Jana was not brought up with airs and graces and did not expect to be spoiled. Until then, she decided to sit back and enjoy the journey, it was hot outside, and she was pleasantly cool in the air-conditioned car.

The limousine turned into a long treelined drive, Jana looked at the palm trees lining the side of the road, she saw a man up one of the trees, he was cutting down some of the foliage. She looked back and saw the most enormous house she had ever seen, the driver pulled up and let her out of the limousine. Jana stood in front of the house and raised her head up as far as she could to look at the size of the house. Just then, the front door opened, an older couple stepped out to greet her. Jana recognised the gentleness of the woman's voice. 'Welcome Jana, it is so nice to meet you, I'm Martha, and this is Charles. We are Charlotte's grandparents. Charlotte has told us so much about you' Martha said.

'Thank you, Martha, how is Charlotte?' Jana asked

'She's taking a nap, she has been eager for you to come, poor thing has worn herself out' Martha replied.

'Come in, come in, I will show you where your room is, and then you can freshen up.' Charles said as he ushered Jana into the house.

Jana stood at the foot of the stairs, she had to raise her head to see the enormous size of the house. Jana saw a woman at the top of the stairs, the woman was smiling down towards Martha and Charles, Jana turned to look at them both and found that they had been watching her with puzzlement on their faces. Jana looked back up the stairs and saw that the woman was gone. 'I am so sorry, this is a magnificent staircase, it took my breath away for a second' Jana said as she apologised for appearing rooted to the spot. Martha laughed' I was the same the first time I saw it too, it is a beautiful staircase, and the workmanship that has gone into it must have been meticulous for the creator.' Martha said as she understood what Jana had meant. They made their way to the room that Jana had been given, 'you are next to Charlotte's room, specific orders from my granddaughter I'm afraid, she would not have it any other way. Charlotte can be quite stubborn at times.' Charles said.

'Charlotte takes after her father; he can be quite stubborn too.' Martha said

'I don't mind being next to Charlotte, she is a lovely little girl, quite charming.' Jana replied.

Jana was in the middle of unpacking her suitcase when there was a knock on her door. Jana answered the door to find Charlotte there, 'oh good you're here' Charlotte said smiling.

'Yes, I'm here' Jana replied ruffling Charlotte's hair. 'Would you like help to get dressed' she asked Charlotte as she could see she was in a dressing gown.

'No, it's ok I have to go and do my water exercises with the nanny.' Charlotte did not have a happy look on her face. As she wheeled herself down the corridor, she turned to Jana 'will you come with me Jana please' she asked.

'Give me five minutes to find my costume, and I will join you' Jana replied, she was concerned that such a young child would have the need to feel so unhappy about someone who is meant to be looking after them. Charlotte smiled and wheeled herself away.

Once dressed, Jana asked for directions from Charles and then made her way to the swimming pool. She got there just in time to see the nanny dropping Charlotte into the pool and Charlotte fighting to keep her head above water. 'What the hell do you think you're doing?' Jana said as she jumped into the pool to help Charlotte. Charlotte was coughing and spluttering as she pulled her to the side. 'What's wrong?' Charles asked as he had heard Jana shouting and came running with Martha to see what the problem was. 'Nothing' the nanny said.

'Nothing, Nothing, don't tell me that was nothing, you stay away from Charlotte do you hear me; don't you ever go near her again' Jana responded with venom in her voice.

'It's my job to look after Charlotte' the nanny retorted.

'If that's your definition of looking after someone, I would hate to see what your definition of loving someone was, now get out before I call the police.' Jana screamed at the nanny.

The nanny turned on her heels and left the room at speed. Turning to Charlotte, she saw that hse was still coughing, 'Martha will you call Charlotte's doctor, please. Charles, can you help me to get her back to her room please.' Jana asked. They both did as they were asked, and Jana settled Charlotte before going to get herself dressed.

'I am so glad you are here Jana', Charlotte said hugging her.

'So am I Charlotte, so am I' Jana replied as she hugged Charlotte back. 'Now you try and get some rest, I'll be in my room getting changed, I won't be far I promise' Jana said encouraging Charlotte to lay back down. Charlotte smiled before closing her eyes. While they waited for the doctor, Jana explained to Charlotte's grandparents what she had seen Sandra do. 'We have never liked that woman; she has always been argumentative and rude.' Martha said. 'You certainly put her in her place.' Charles said chuckling, the telephone rang, and he went to answer it, 'I suggest you come home and deal with the situation instead of hiding behind that big desk, it's time you took responsibility for that woman.' Charles said before hanging the phone up abruptly.

Martha was concerned now she could see the anger in Charles's face when he came back into the room. 'Is everything alright dear' Martha asked, she had not seen him like this for some years. 'Yes, Yes, I feel that everything is going to be very good from now on' he said, looking over toward Jana. Just then the doctor arrived, Charles answered the door and showed him up into Charlotte's room, Jana explained to him what had happened. The doctor was a gentleman, as he walked in, he smiled and nodded in response to Jana's explanation. 'My what has been happening to you, young lady' he said, smiling at Charlotte as he walked towards her. Charlotte smiled back and hugged the doctor as if they were old friends. 'come on let's listen to that chest of yours, we need to make sure there is no water in your lungs eh.' He said as he pulled out his stethoscope. Jana stood back with Martha and Charles to let the doctor do his job.

The doctor continued to talk to Charlotte throughout his assessment of her and pulling a toffee out of his pocket gave it to her, ruffling her hair he said, 'you are going to be a fine young lady, but I am going to give you some medicine to help you.' Charlotte nodded as she took the sweet from him and popped it into her mouth. Jana promised to come back after seeing the doctor to the door, 'It was a good job you called me, Charlotte has a start of an infection going on in her lungs, I am going to send over a bottle of antibiotic medication for her. It's a time-specific antibiotic so please make sure she takes it at the right time. Jana thanked the doctor, once he had left, she turned to Martha and Charles and apologised, for taking over the situation. They both smiled at Jana, 'it is a good job you did so, maybe Brandon will listen to Charlotte now.' Martha said.

'Speaking of Brandon,' Charles interrupted 'it was him on the phone earlier. Apparently, the nanny had rung him to complain about the way you treated her Jana'.

'The way I treated her, what about the way she treated Charlotte, the cheek of the woman. Who does she think she is treating a child like that?'

Jana could feel the anger mounting up again and excused herself to go and check on Charlotte. Opening Charlotte's bedroom door quietly, she looked around, she saw that Charlotte was fast asleep. Jana also saw a woman standing over Charlotte and was about to tell her to get out thinking it was the nanny when the woman turned to her and smiled before vanishing. Jana was used to seeing spirit now and realised that it was the same woman that had been on the stairs when she had come into the house. Jana had a feeling of who the woman was, Jana was not one, however, to jump to conclusions and made a mental note to try to find out who she was. Jana closed the door quietly and returned to the drawing-room where Martha and Charles, was getting ready for some afternoon tea. Martha was quite an inquisitive woman and reminded Jana of Rachel. Martha quizzed Jana on her life and where Jana had met Charlotte and her father. Jana explained how she had met them; they began to laugh as they imagined Brandon crossing his legs, desperate to go to the toilet.

While they chatted, Charles lifted his head, 'the chopper is coming' he said as he got up to go outside. 'That can mean only one thing, Brandon' Martha said to Jana.

'Your right and he does not look happy' Charles said as he watched the chopper land through his binoculars. It was not long before, Brandon entered the room and demanded to know what the hell was going on. Jana did not take lightly to his tone and getting up to shut the door that he had left open, swung back around on her heels to face him.

'If you are referring to the situation with the nanny, then I would ask that you give me the chance to explain it to you before you go biting everyone's heads off here' Jana said as she gestured towards Charles and Martha. Jana was ready for him; who did he think he was coming into the room like that? How rude she thought.

Martha had to turn away from Brandon for fear of his seeing her smile, she knew that it would infuriate him. Marth also felt that he had met his match in Jana. 'Well, I'm waiting for an explanation' Brandon said.

'Then you had better sit down and show some manners Charles said to Brandon. He had never spoken to his son-in-law like this before, it was about time he had a piece of his mind. Shocked at the way his father-in-law had talked to him, Brandon did as he was told. Jana took over from Charles, 'I wonder whose life you value more Brandon, is it your daughters or the nanny?' Jana asked directly.

'What kind of question in that?' Brandon demanded to know. Not perturbed by his arrogant manner, Jana continued to question him.

'How much research did you do on your nanny, or did you just take the first one that came along' Jana demanded to know. She could see he was getting angry, his cheeks had become inflamed, and his jaw was gritted tightly together.

Brandon stood up and walked over to look out of the window. Knowing that he would have to pull himself together and calm down before he answered Jana, he caught his breath and turning back towards her, Brandon said. 'how I conduct my business of finding an appropriate nanny for Charlotte is nothing to do with you' he said in a frustratingly calm manner.

'I believe it is my business, I think the moment you asked me to come and look after Charlotte you made it my business.' 'If you can't or won't answer my questions, then I am afraid that I cannot stay here to look after Charlotte. I refuse to work with a nanny who abuses children' Jana said in an equally abrupt manner. 'I shall go and pack my bags, I am sure you won't mind me saying goodbye to Charlotte on my way out, please call me a Taxi Charles.' Jana said as she left the room.

'Don't you dare call a cab; this is not over yet' Brandon shouted to Charles as he followed Jana through the door.

Charles looked at Martha, shaking her head; she said, 'they will sort it out between them, there is no need for the taxi.'

'He had better sort it out, it is about time he took responsibility of Charlotte himself.

'Brandon has been hiding behind work and has not been giving enough attention to the child since her mother died.' Charles said with tears in his eyes at the memory of losing his daughter. Brandon caught up with Jana, reaching out he grabbed her arm, only to pull back his hand as he suddenly realised that her arm was false. Jana could see the look on his face and said, 'don't worry, I won't hit you with it, even though you make me so mad I want to.

' Please, Jana could we start again?' Brandon knew that he needed to keep Jana on his side, Charlotte had been so insistent that Jana was the one to look after her. *"I like having her around as well, I have never known a woman to stand up to me the way Jana has,"* Brandon thought to himself. 'Yes, we can, but only if you keep that stinking attitude of yours to yourself.' Jana said with determination in her voice.

Brandon promised to keep a more civil tongue in his head through gritted teeth and held himself together. He then showed Jana into the conservatory, Jana could see the magnificent garden through the French doors. Seeing Jana's eyes light up at the scene, Brandon opened the doors and asked her to take a seat on the cast iron garden furniture just on the green in front of them. He offered her a refreshing cold drink before pursuing her for more information. Jana explained what had happened and how she had found Charlotte fighting to keep her head above water. Brandon stood up and walked out of the room, thanking Jana for her honesty and asked her to stay where she was before leaving. Martha and Charles came into the room shortly after and asked what Brandon had said. Jana explained that he had not said anything other than asking her to stay just before he left. Jana excused herself and went to her room. Jana could hear Charlotte chatting away, as she passed her room, thinking that she was talking to her father, Jana went to her own room to finish unpacking her things.

There was a veranda outside her window, grabbing her book Jana went to sit out in the fresh air. Jana could hear, Charlotte giggling and chatting away, she must love her father very much, she thought to herself. As she listened, Jana heard Brandon chatting and realised that he was in the garden when she heard Charles talking to him. Puzzled as to who Charlotte was talking to, Jana knocked on her door, she heard Charlotte say 'quick go before they see you' she then told Jana to come into the room. 'Hello sweetie, how are you?' Jana said, putting her hand to Charlotte's forehead to see if she was still feeling hot.

'Hi Jana, I'm feeling better, thank you' Charlotte replied.

'Who were you talking to?' Jana asked Charlotte

'No-one, I was just talking to myself. Was that my daddy I heard?' Charlotte asked trying to distract Jana from asking further questions.

'Yes, he said he would be up to see you soon,' Jana knew Brandon did not say so, but she believed in her heart that he would. 'I'll be right back' Jana said before leaving to get Charlotte a drink and something to eat.

Jana went down into the kitchen where she found cupboards full of food, there was nothing a child could snack on except fruit, and although Jana herself felt that it was good to eat healthily, she also believed that a child should be entitled to a treat now and then. Jana asked Martha if she would take the drink to Charlotte, 'I'm going to go into the village to get Charlotte a treat' she said.

'It's quite a walk to the village' Martha said.

'That's ok I like to walk' Jana said as she headed out for the door. Jana looked back toward the house as she walked down the drive, it did not appear to get any smaller, despite her getting further away from it. She was not walking long before a car pulled up beside her. Martha had sent Charles to take her into town. 'I could have walked' Jana said, getting into the car. 'One thing I have learned over the years and that is not to argue with Martha, she will always win. Martha thinks Charlotte gets her stubbornness from her father. I think she gets it from Martha' Charles said with a wink.

They both laughed, and Jana thanked him for the lift. 'I heard you talking to Brandon earlier and things getting a bit heated. Is everything ok?' Jana asked Charles.

'Yes, everything is fine, I just needed to get a lot of things off my chest, I have been bottling it up for years' Charles replied.

'Is there anything I can help you with?' Jana asked

'You already have dear, you in one moment have opened up my eyes and heart, I would like to thank you for that.' Charles said. Jana had no idea what he meant but smiled anyway. They continued the journey into the village in quiet. Charles stopped the car by the local shop, as they walked in Jana spotted a stuffed rabbit with big green eyes and floppy ears, and in his feet, he was holding a large bar of chocolate. *"That's the perfect gift for Charlotte,"* Jana thought to herself. Charles watched her as she purchased the rabbit and placed it carefully into a gift bag. 'Would you like to go for a glass of wine? I'd like to talk to you if I may' Charles asked. 'Of course, that would be nice, thank you' Jana replied.

Charles took her to a local tavern, while he went to the bar Jana took the opportunity to look around the place. The room was warm, there was no air conditioning, and it had a musty smell to it. Jana was glad of the chilled wine that Charles placed before her. 'What is it you wanted to talk to me about Charles?' Jana asked.

'I would like to apologise for the way my Son-In-Law has spoken to you today, he has been insulting. I have indeed told him what I think, he was not happy, but as I say I have bottled up too much over the years. It was about time I said something to him' Charles said.

'I appreciate the apology Charles, but don't you think it should be coming from Brandon?' Jana asked.

'Yes, yes, of course, I do, but I also know that Brandon is a stubborn man, and very seldom does he apologise to anyone. I'm afraid he has been like this since his wife and parents died' Charles said.

Before Jana could ask him, what had happened, Charles thanked her for helping his granddaughter, 'If you had not been there today, I don't know what would have happened' Charles said his voice shaking. I do hope my Son-in-law sees you for the kind person that you are, and how good you will be for Charlotte, he smiled and caught hold of Jana's' hand as he spoke. 'I hope Brandon sees sense and gets rid of that nanny; she was so cruel to Charlotte. I don't think I will be able to stay if she is going to stay here' Jana said with complete honesty.

'Brandon has reassured me that she will be fired and that he is going to furthermore report her to the police' Charles said. Jana smiled a knowing smile after they finished their drink, they returned to the car and made their way back to the house.

When they returned, Jana found Charlotte in the conservatory with Martha. 'You should be resting little missy' Jana said to Charlotte with a playful scowl on her face.

'I am resting, I promise. I've been chatting to granny, but I am resting' she said as she tried to stretch her neck around to see what Jana was hiding behind her back.

'What's that behind your back?' she asked Jana

'What's what?' Jana replied, turning around in a circle as if to look for what Charlotte was seeing. Charlotte began to laugh a hearty laugh, and her grandmother started to cry.

Chapter Seven:
Charlie's Golden Rules

Martha excused herself and left the room, Charles followed her out of the room, hugging Martha he asked if she was alright. 'Oh Charles, I have not heard the child laugh like that for a long time, not since her mother was alive.' Martha said as she was unable to hold back the tears of the memories of her daughter and granddaughter playing together came flooding back. 'Come on, let's get you a cup of tea to calm your nerves,' Charles said, leading her to the kitchen. None of them had seen Brandon in the doorway and was not aware that he had seen Charlotte laughing and heard their conversation about it. Brandon walked into the room as Jana gave Charlotte her gift. Charlotte turned to her father 'look daddy look what Jana has given me, isn't he beautiful' she said hugging the rabbit.

'Yes, darling it is' he said, picking both Charlotte and the rabbit up to hug them.

'Charlie, will you be alright for a while, I need to talk the grown-up talk with Jana, ok.'

Brandon placed Charlotte back down on the sofa. 'Daddy, you always treat me like a baby, I'm a big girl now, aren't I Jana' Charlotte said

'Yes, of course, you are, we won't be long, ok' Jana replied as she smiled and ruffled charlottes hair.

'Ok, you can call me Charlie like daddy does if you want Jana' Charlotte shouted as they left the room.

'You seem to have a good rapport with my daughter Jana' Brandon said

'Yes, I do, is there a problem with that?' Jana became defensive.

'No not at all, I just wanted to thank you for helping Charlotte today. I did not realise that the nanny was like that with her, and yes, you are right. I should have had the nanny vetted more before hiring her' Brandon said.

'So, what will happen with the nanny now?' Jana asked concerned that she might be employed to look after other children.

'I have reported her to the police, it is in their hands now. I don't think she will be looking after children after this.' Brandon reassured Jana.

Brandon became quiet as he prepared himself to ask Jana to work for him. 'Right now, I have a proposition for you. I would like to employ you to look after Charlotte, she is very fond of you, and as my in-laws have pointed out, you are perfect for Charlotte.'

'Do I get some time to think about it, I will have my own rules that cannot be questioned' Jana said sternly.

'Of course, make me a list, and we shall go through them in the morning' Brandon said before he excused himself, saying he needed to be making some business calls. Jana returned to Charlotte and her grandparents, who were sitting with her by this time. 'Granny and grandad have to go home soon; I shall be all alone' Charlotte said with tears running down her face. 'You won't be alone, Jana is here with you, and we will be back soon enough' Martha said stroking Charlotte's hair.

Looking at Jana with puppy dog eyes charlotte began pleading with her. 'Will you Jana, will you, will you please' she asked, repeating herself.

'yes, I will. I will stay for a while, there is one condition. I have rules that you must follow. Is that alright with you, Charlotte' Jana asked. Charlotte's brows came together as she frowned. Her grandparents began to laugh, knowing full well that Charlotte did not like rules. Charlotte thought for a while before answering, 'what rules?' she asked.

'Well, I thought we could make them together, that is me you and your grandparents because I know they only want what is best for you. I also know little madam that you are sometimes very naughty for them' Jana said. Charlotte appeared shocked by this statement.

'How do you know?' she asked Jana.

'oh, I know' Jana replied winking at her.

It was time for their evening meal, and they had been called to the dining room where a table had been set, and the meal was ready for them to eat. Charlotte was eager to tell her father of the rules. Brandon, however, was not too keen on Charlotte being involved in the decision making of her own rules. 'Well that is one of the rules that cannot be questioned, and so the choice is yours to make Brandon' Jana said. Brandon frowned in the same way that Charlotte had earlier, and everyone around him burst into laughter. 'What's the matter, why is everyone laughing' Brandon asked

'Daddy you do pull such funny faces sometimes' Charlotte said laughing. The whole table began to roar with laughter. Brandon continued to frown, which in turn made everyone around him laugh even louder. They all settled to eat their meal, and Jana promised to sit with Charlotte and her grandparents after the meal to put together the rules. Right young lady, Jana said as they finished their meals, time for those rules. Charles and Martha got up to go first, with Jana and Charlotte following behind, as they did so Brandon got to his feet as if to follow.

Immediately Charlotte said 'not you daddy, this has to be our rules' she began to laugh as again a frown appeared on Brandon's brow. 'Well I shall have to agree with them Charlie, you know that don't you' he replied sternly.

'of course, I do daddy' Charlotte replied, smiling. Once settled Charlotte began to say what the rules were going to be. Shaking her head at her, Jana said 'I don't think so young lady you are here to have input only'. Charles and Martha laughed as they saw the same expression and frown over Charlotte's brow as they had her father's moments ago. Pouting, Charlotte asked how many rules were there going to be? And if she could name her own rules, laughing the adults agreed that Charlotte could give the rules a name herself. 'then they shall be called Charlie's golden rules' said Charlotte with a big smile.

Jana asked Martha, Charles and Charlotte to think about things that were to be the most important of the rules. 'School' Martha said firmly 'Charlotte has missed so much school, I'm afraid she will never catch up' she said with concern. All the while, Charles was nodding in agreement. 'Alright, then the first rule is school.' Charlotte gave her famous pout. 'secondly, I think that Charlotte should continue with her pool exercises after school', Jana said. Charlotte immediately retorted this, saying that she would not be going in the pool again with a nanny. Jana reassured her that any hydrotherapy would be done with Jana herself. 'what's that?' Charlotte asked with a puzzled look on her face.

Jana explained that this was exercises in the pool to help Charlotte to strengthen her muscles in her legs. 'oh, the same as I was doing with the nanny then' Charlotte said.

'no, the nanny only had you to try and kick your legs in the water' Jana replied.

'I will be setting up an exercise regime, especially for your needs' Jana said with confidence. 'Now the third and final rule, should Charlotte follow the rules one and two, then rule three should be that Charlotte chooses the family holiday' Said Jana.

'yes' Charlotte said, punching the air in excitement. 'We must all go on the family holiday' Charlotte said looking directly at Martha and Charles, before turning towards Jana, 'you as well Jana' Charlotte said sternly.

'well, we will see' Jana replied, smiling at the young girl.

'ok, let's go through the rules again' Charlotte was excited and glad there were only three.

Charlotte must attend school

Charlotte must do hydrotherapy daily after school

Charlotte gets to choose the family holidays

'Let's go and tell daddy' Charlotte said excitingly, and they all went to see if they could find Brandon.

They found Brandon sitting in the garden staring out into the distance, it was a few seconds before he realised that they were all standing there watching him. Jumping slightly, he smiled at Charlotte and told her she had scared him witless; Charlotte began to give a belly laugh as she found the thought of her father being scared by her funny. 'Daddy, we have finished the rules' said Charlotte excitedly

'oh, you have, have you' he replied with a smile on his face 'let's hear them then.'

'well… Charlotte began to read off the list, and as Brandon listened, he nodded in agreement until Charlotte came to the third rule by which he lifted his eyes to the adults around him and said 'I hope you realised what you have done, she is going to want to go to Disney Land.' Charlotte began clapping her hands 'yes, daddy, yes. I was thinking the same thing' Charlotte reached over out of her wheelchair and pulling at her father's arms began hugging him tightly.

Martha, Charles and Jana broke into uncontrollable laughter, Jana saying through the laughter 'you must follow the other two rules.'

'I will Jana, I promise' Charlotte said as she yawned.

'time for bed for you' Martha said as she began to turn the chair around to take Charlotte to her room.

'will you come and tuck me in Jana please' charlotte shouted over her shoulder.

'I will be up soon' Jana promised. Brandon offered Charles and Jana a drink. 'No thank you, I am going to go up and read Charlotte a story' Charles said before leaving them both in the warmth of the night.

Handing Jana, a glass of wine, Brandon smiled and said he was surprised that there were no more than three rules for Charlotte to follow. 'Less is more' Jana said as she explained that it was more important to get Charlotte back into a routine. 'she needs her friends around her' she said as she remembered what it was like to be an only child.

They sat for some time, both staring out into the distance. Brandon wondering what was going on in Jana's head and Jana thinking the same about Brandon. Her drink was finished, and Jana stood up and said goodnight to Brandon, he stood up to say goodnight, as Jana walked away, he said 'thank you, Jana'

'what for' Jana asked in a puzzled voice

'for putting the smile back on my daughter's face,' he replied with sorrow in his eyes. Jana nodded and took herself off to tuck Charlotte into bed. As Jana walked up the stairs, she could hear Charlotte crying. The closer she got to the door, the more she could feel the pain in her voice. 'it is my fault, if I had not been naughty, it would not have happened' Charlotte said through the tears.

'no, my darling, it was an accident, nothing more' Jana could hear a woman talking to Charlotte. As she walked closer, she could see that the door had been left ajar, looking in Jana again saw the same woman she had seen before on the stairs and in Charlotte's room previously.

Suddenly the woman vanished, Charlotte tried to wipe away the tears not for Jana to see them. 'who was the lady you were talking to Charlotte?' Jana asked.

'I wasn't talking to anyone; I must have been dreaming' Charlotte replied. Jana decided not to question it any; further, obviously Charlotte was distraught, she felt it would be better left for another day. Tucking Charlotte in Jana kissed her on the forehead and said goodnight, making a promise to herself to get to the bottom of what was bothering Charlotte. Jana decided to go for a swim and returned to her room to change into her costume. As she entered her room, she could see the all too familiar ball of light swirling around. 'come on, show yourself' Jana said, smiling to herself. It was only when her angel appeared that she saw the second ball of light. 'who's your friend?' she asked her angel.

'all in good time Jana, when the time is right, and you are ready you will find out' her angel replied. 'I have been asked to tell you to tread carefully with Charlotte, she is tormented by what has happened and will need you to be very patient with her' Jana's angel said looking towards the ball of light when speaking.

Jana believed that she already knew who the spirit was. The angel smiled at her knowingly as if to confirm her suspicions. 'Be careful little one, you open up your heart too easily and get yourself hurt in the process, be careful' the angel repeated before vanishing. Jana was puzzled at what her angel had said and decided to leave thinking over what had been told until later. She changed into her costume and headed down to the pool, on her way down, she met Charles, who had been coming to look for her. 'Be careful Jana' he begged as he explained that the nanny had been on the phone, making all sorts of threats towards Jana.

'please do not worry about me Charles, I am capable of looking after myself' Jana said with a smile. Charles smiled back and headed off in the opposite direction to Jana. Charles found his wife reading a book in the library. 'that is one angry woman' he said

'Who?' Maratha asked

'that nanny' he replied.

'Why, what is wrong?' Martha asked. Charles proceeded to tell her about the threats that the nanny had made about Jana. 'Don't worry about Jana, she is one feisty young lady' Martha responded chuckling to herself.

Martha had seen how she had handled Brandon and knew that Jana would be a force to be reckoned with. Neither Martha nor Charles had seen Brandon in the doorway, he slipped away so that they did not notice him. Brandon felt hurt and betrayed by his In-Laws. *"Why would they think that Jana would need to be defensive towards me? Do they consider me a monster?"* he thought to himself. Brandon decided to look for Jana and confront her, believing that she,

Martha and Charles had been talking about him behind his back. Brandon was ready to have it out with Jana when he found her swimming in the pool. What he saw, stopped him in his tracks; he had forgotten about Jana's arm. Realising that there was just a stump and not the prosthetic limb that Brandon had become used to seeing, made him lose his train of thought. He watched Jana swimming for a while from in the shadows. Brandon could not shake the feeling about her, and Jana's arm kept bothering him, although Brandon could not figure out why. He had been so busy with work and the nanny situation that he did not realise the situation arising before him.

Brandon left the pool with Jana not even knowing that he was there, he was practically running to his study and thought he would have to be a little devious himself. Brandon believed he had an idea who Jana was and knew that he would have to be gentle to get the truth out of her. Brandon poured himself a drink, feeling angry himself, believing that Jana was the one who was being deceitful in not telling him who she really was. Brandon picked up the telephone and called Richard Wilson, the private investigator he had hired to find the woman who saved his Brother Cullum's life. The phone rang out for a while before it was answered. 'Hello, Richard Wilson, private investigator.' Brandon did not give him a chance to say anything further before bellowing down the telephone 'where the hell have you been?' Richard could hear the anger in Brandon's voice and chose not to answer the question for fear of repercussion. 'How can I help you?' Richard asked.

'You can give me a description of the woman who I hired you to find' Brandon said with anger in his tone.

'I have tried to explain to you, she refuses to see you. I cannot force her to see you' Richard said.

Brandon was getting very impatient; he was not used to people not telling him what he wanted to know. 'just send me a description of her' he yelled before putting the phone down on the private investigator. Brandon went over and turned on his computer, he knew that Richard would be typing up the email to him immediately. He began to pace the room impatiently with a drink in his hand. Finally, the email had arrived, he was sat at the computer when Jana knocked on the study door, she was hoping she could get some information about Charlotte's condition so that she could put the exercise regime together for her. 'Come in, take a seat' Brandon said, trying to keep the civil tongue that he promised her he would. 'How can I help you? he asked.

'I need to know about Charlotte's condition so that I will be able to set up an appropriate exercise program' Jana said.

'Exercise programme, don't you think that should be left to the experts' Brandon replied sarcastically.

'well if you want to pay extortionate rates to help her that's your choice, the offer will still be there if you need it' Jana said in an equally sarcastic tone. How dare he she thought to herself, was he saying that she was not professional enough for his daughter. With that, she got up and stormed out of the room.

Brandon picked up the phone and called the private detective again. 'I have a job for you. I want you to find out Jana Heart's background.

'yes sir' he replied before slamming the phone down, it was his turn to be sarcastic now he liked Jana, and he was getting fed up at being treated like a worthless piece of meat by Brandon. It would take some time for the investigator to get the information he needed, and Brandon knew he would have to continue to remain calm until he knew everything he needed to know about Jana. By the time he had finished speaking to the private investigator, everyone had gone to bed. As Brandon walked up the stairs, both Charlotte and Jana were screaming in their sleep. By the time he had reached the top of the stairs Martha was in comforting Charlotte and Charles was hovering at Jana's door not knowing what to do. Brandon opened the door to find Jana writhing around in her bed and slowly walked towards her.

Jana woke suddenly to find him hovering over her bed, she began sobbing uncontrollably into his shoulder. Brandon looked towards his father-in-law who just shrugged his shoulders in response. He never said a word to Jana, he just sat there holding her close letting her release all her tears over his shirt. Jana was calmer by the time Martha came into the room.

'Charlotte is asking for you' she told Brandon as she took in the scene. 'I'll take over here' she said shoving both men out of the room. 'Are you alright, Jana?' Martha asked. Jana was embarrassed at the scene she had caused and apologised to Martha.

'Do not be silly' Martha said, 'we all get bad dreams sometimes, have you had these dreams before?' She asked.

'yes, I get them quite a lot' Jana replied

'would you like to talk about them?' said Martha.

'I'm sorry, could we leave it for tonight, and I'll explain it to you tomorrow' Jana asked

'Of course, of course, you get some rest now do you hear' Martha said in a stern motherly voice.

Martha left Jana to rest and went to seek out Charles and Brandon. Martha found them in the study discussing what had happened. 'It appears we have two tormented souls in the house now' Martha said. 'was Charlotte dreaming about the crash again' Brandon asked Martha.

'yes, and I don't think it is going to get any easier for her any time soon' Martha replied. They decided to have a hot drink before bed, and all headed to the kitchen. Brandon then asked about Jana. 'did Jana tell you what she was screaming about' he asked Martha.

'No, the poor thing is exhausted, I told her to get some rest and that we would talk tomorrow' she said. The hot drinks in their hands, both Martha and Charles went to bed. It was still warm, and so Brandon sat out in the garden wondering what had happened, why had Jana had such a bad nightmare?

Morning came, and Jana woke with a splitting headache, she reached for her bag to get some pain relief, before laying back down for a while, giving the pain a chance to recede. It was the middle of the morning before she woke, she showered and dressed then made her way downstairs to find Charlotte whizzing around in her wheelchair, laughing hysterically as her father was on all fours chasing her. They watched as Jana came down the stairs, 'good morning sleepy head' Charlotte said jokingly.

'good morning' she replied a little sheepishly. Brandon never said a word he just stood there with a grin on his face.

'nanny and grandad are going home today' Charlotte said with disappointment in her tone.

'they will soon be back; they just have to deal with some business' Brandon told Charlotte ruffling her hair as he did so.

Martha and Charles had entered the room at this point and reassured Charlotte that they would indeed be returning, promising that they would be there for her tenth birthday. Charlotte smiled and leaning out of her chair gave them both a big hug, they both bent down to kiss Charlotte on the cheek and hug her back. Their car had pulled up outside the front door, Brandon helped put the cases in the car before hugging his in-law's goodbye. They all stood and watched as the vehicle drove away. Charlotte began to cry, she loved her grandparents dearly, and when they were there, she felt closer to her mother. 'come on, let's get some ice cream' Brandon said, trying to distract her.

'yes, lets' Jana said, smiling at Charlotte.

It was Charlottes time to look sheepish, and her father knew all too well what the look was about. Brandon did not want to upset her any further and said quickly 'let's go onto the town and have a meal with ice-cream for afters.' Jana looked at him with a puzzled look on her face. 'can Jana come as well please' Charlotte asked her father giving him a big cheesy smile as if trying to encourage him to let her come.

'of course, she can silly' he replied.

'yes' Charlotte said clapping her hands as hard as she could to make a loud clapping noise. They were in the car when Charlotte decided she wanted to go to the beach for her ice-cream. Laughing, her father agreed, and they headed towards the shore. Secretly Jana was grateful for going there, after her nightmare she felt the need to be close to her loved ones. They parked up and found a seat before Brandon went off to buy the ice-cream. 'you madam are spoilt' Jana said to Charlotte laughing as she said it. Charlotte smiled in response.

Jana looked over toward Brandon, as she did so, her stomach did summersaults. She already thought Brandon was a good-looking man, this morning however she realised just how good looking he was. He had stubble across his rugged chin, and the worry lines had left his face, giving him a softer look. Jana longed to kiss his lips as if sensing her looking Brandon turned around and looked her directly in the eyes, Jana looked away sharply her cheeks aflame with embarrassment. He had not missed her blushing and wondered what she had been thinking. Jana felt too embarrassed to speak and sat in silence eating her ice-cream, before getting up and kicking off her shoes, she needed to have the comforting feel of the sea on her feet more now than ever. As she ran down the beach to the sea, she saw her angel again. Her angel did not say anything, just smiled and pointed back towards Charlotte and her father.

Jana turned to look at what the angel was pointing at, only to find that Brandon has picked charlotte up out of her wheelchair and was following her down to the sea, Charlotte was laughing loudly and was attracting stares from strangers, the more they stared, the more she laughed. They soon reached Jana; Brandon could not seem to stop himself; he had been running so hard to catch up with her. Splash… they both ended up in the sea. Jana watched in horror as Brandon picked Charlotte up out of the sea, their clothes and hair dripping everywhere, they both looked at each other and then looked at Jana and burst out laughing at the shocked expression on Jana's face. Jana was not amused 'you could have both been hurt' she said with concern. Brandon saw the fear on her face and stopped laughing, he apologised to Jana and promised that it was an accident. Charlotte kept on laughing as she continued to see the funny side of it.

Brandon always kept a spare bag of clothes for himself in his car as he was always rushing off at one time or another, but they needed to buy new clothes for Charlotte, Brandon handed over his credit card and asked if Jana would go and buy some for her. Brandon carried Charlotte back to the car and wrapped a car blanket around her until Jana returned with her clothes. Jana went to the nearest clothes shop; she did not want Charlotte to get a chill and needed to get the clothes back to her as quickly as she could. Jana was so annoyed with Brandon for dropping his daughter into the sea. 'Why does he have to make me feel so uptight all the time?' Jana thought to herself. She could not understand how her emotions were so up and down. Jana realised that she had no idea what kind of clothes Charlotte liked.

As she looked around the clothes, she saw a ball of light bouncing around by some dresses. Jana was aware that it did not belong to her angel. She believed it was Charlotte's mother showing her what she would like to see her daughter wearing, she did not see her spirit, it felt more like a knowing. How Jana knew remained a mystery to her. Something she hoped she would so be able to discover for herself. Jana made her purchases of the clothes as fast as possible and made her way back to Brandon and Charlotte. She found them chatting as she approached them, Brandon turned to look at her, suddenly turning his head away again. Jana had not missed the fact that he had wiped some tears away. Jana did not show Brandon that she had seen him, rather than embarrass him, she pulled out the clothes for Charlotte and swung them in front of her face teasing her, as she tried to grab the clothes Charlotte began to giggle wholeheartedly. 'oh, you are so funny Jana' she said through the giggles.

Jana helped her get dressed, Charlotte loved her new clothes and gave Jana a big hug as her father watched on with tears in his eyes. Jana looked towards the heavens and gave a silent thank you to Charlotte's mother. 'Come on she said let's go and get that meal, you both must be hungry by now?' Jana said.

'Famished, Jana' Brandon replied with a smile on his face.

'Can we have pizza, can we can we, please….' Charlotte asked again with a cheesy grin on her face.

'Um, what do you think? Brandon' Jana asked winking at him. Brandon looked down at his daughter with a stern look upon his face, he could not hold the gaze for long as he burst into laughter, looking at his daughter's cheesy grin. Tickling her, he nodded his head. 'Oh, thank you, daddy, thank you, Jana,' Charlotte said, smiling. Jana thought how well-mannered the little girl was, how well she had been brought up by her family.

They found a fast food shop selling pizza, the girls sat at the table by the window while Brandon went and ordered the food. Charlotte looked up towards the sky and told Jana that her mummy was in heaven. 'How do you know?' Jana asked as she watched the little girl looking up at the sky; as if hoping to get a glimpse of her mother. Charlotte was about to answer her when her father came back. Instead, Charlotte gestured towards her mouth and pretended to turn an imaginary key. They all chatted as they ate, soon Charlotte was yawning, they finished up their food and headed home. Charlotte was fast asleep within minutes of being in the car. It was not long before they were back home, Brandon carried his daughter up to her bedroom, he placed her on the bed and took her shoes off. Placing her blankets over her, Brandon kissed her goodnight. Jana watched as he left the room and smiling, followed him onto the landing. Jana could see the love Brandon had for Charlotte.

Brandon turned to her and pulling her towards him, holding her close he said, 'Thank you for a wonderful day, Jana. Thank you for putting the smile back on Charlotte's face.' Brandon let her go as suddenly as he had grabbed her and walked off. Jana did not know what happened why he had let go of her so abruptly or why he was leaving. Brandon made his way to his study and poured himself a whiskey, placing the glass to his lips and drinking the whiskey down in one go. He could feel it burning the back of his throat as he poured himself another one. Angry with himself; Brandon knew he was attracted to Jana but could not allow this to happen. He loved his wife dearly, he could not soil her memory like that, and then there was Charlotte. Brandon had to think about his daughter, she was still grieving over her mother. Charlotte missed her so badly, and he would often hear his daughter crying herself to sleep. *"No,"* he thought *"I can't do that to her, not while she remains so tormented"* his thoughts were racing, and it took some time for him to calm himself down.

Brandon paced around his study, occasionally leaning against the top of his large oak desk, tapping his fingers on his glass. Several hours had passed, he opened the French doors leading from his study to the gardens and saw that it was almost dawn. Brandon knew that consuming too much alcohol had affected him and did not want Charlotte to see him this way. There was only one thing he could do, he called his secretary and arranged for a helicopter to pick him up. Brandon left a note for Jana telling her that he had been called away urgently to work, asking her to relay the message to Charlotte for him. His company had offices and apartments all over the world. There was one in Madrid, he would go there. Brandon had been working more and more from home since the death of his wife, leaving Charlotte in the capable hands of her grandparents when there was a work emergency. This was different, this time he felt guilty about lying to her.

It was not long before the helicopter was picking up and he was flying towards Madrid. Back at the house, Jana was again thrashing around in her sleep. Jana began dreaming, this time, it was more intense than before. The faceless man had her by the arms, he was shaking her violently. 'Where is it? Where is it?' he was shouting at Jana with venom in his tone.

'I don't know what you're talking about' she replied.

'Liar' He said. He screamed, so hard that she could feel his saliva land on her face as he shouted. His voice became quieter as it drifted off into the distance, Jana could hear someone calling out her name, she tried to see where the shouting was coming from, realising it was not part of the dream she woke with a jolt, there was sweat running off her face, and her bedclothes were sodden. She was scared, the visions were getting more lifelike every time she had one. Jana heard her name being called again; it was Charlotte. She got up, put her dressing gown on and went to see what was wrong.

Charlotte was still in bed; she was sobbing bitterly. 'What's the matter Charlotte?' Jana said, sitting down beside her, she lifted the child towards her, they both needed a hug at this time. Jana tried to sooth Charlotte; it took a while for her to calm down, when she could eventually speak, Charlotte told her that she been dreaming about her father and that he had gone. She said to Jana that everyone was looking for him, but no one could find him. Charlotte began to sob again. 'Come on, let me get dressed, and I will get you in your wheelchair, then we can look for him. I'm sure he's in the kitchen making breakfast' Jana said trying to distract the child from the horrid thoughts. She laid Charlotte back down, 'I won't be long' Jana said reassuring the child, leaving the door ajar before she left. While showering Jana wondered why Brandon had not responded to his daughter calling him, *"Maybe he's listening to music"* Jana thought.

Jana got dressed and returned to Charlotte, as she reached the door, she could hear her talking and thinking it was Brandon Jana waited outside the door, not to disturb them. 'I had a bad dream' Jana could here Charlotte explaining what had happened. 'What was the dream about?' It was a woman's voice Jana could hear; she looked through the child's bedroom door and saw the woman she believed to be Charlotte's mother, Jana listened to the conversation between mother and daughter.

'It was about daddy; he was missing, and no one can find him' Charlotte said.

'I am sure he is fine my little snowdrop' said the woman, turning to look at Jana she smiled and then she was gone. Charlotte sighed as she left. Jana waited for a few seconds before entering the room, she was used to seeing spirit by now but wondered why Charlotte continued to see the spirit of her dead mother. As she entered the child's room, she said to her in a joyful voice, 'Are you ready, to go daddy hunting?'

'Oh-you can be so funny, Jana' Charlotte said as she began to laugh.

Jana helped her to dress, she put a cute yellow daisy print summer dress and yellow sandals on charlotte. 'Now, how are we going to get you into your chair? With you not being able to move your legs and me with one arm, it's going to be difficult' Jana said.

'You are silly, bring my chair to the side of the bed' Charlotte instructed. Jana did as she was told and with the chair placed in its position, she watched as Charlotte rolled herself over, then pulled herself around until her back was facing the chair.

'Right, you hold me and help me into the chair now.' Jana did as she was told but felt nervous, she did not want the child to fall, *"What if she misses the chair?"* she thought.

'Come on, come on, I want to find daddy' Charlotte said, becoming impatient.

Jana looked at Charlotte and saw the two familiar lights bobbing around the child's head, she felt more comfortable now she knew that she had divine support. Charlotte, now safe in her chair began to wheel herself to the door, 'Now, now, slow down little missy' Jana said taking the handles of the chair and guiding her safely through the bedroom door.

Searching for Brandon, Jana had a sudden thought, she needed to contact Rachel or Louise, she knew they would only worry about her. Jana left herself a mental note to do so a little later, she pushed Charlotte into the kitchen. There was no sign of Brandon in the kitchen; they went to the study to look for him, Brandon was not there either. *"Where could he be?"* Jana thought. It was not like him not to be around when his daughter was screaming in her sleep. She looked in the study and finding a note on the desk, Jana read it aloud for charlotte to hear. She expected her to be upset, but Charlotte responded to the news in a calm manner 'Work again' she said before shrugging her shoulders. Jana, however, did not feel that she could calm down. *"How dare he? How dare he just leave his child like that,"* she thought. One thing Jana knew was that Brandon certainly knew how to wind her up and make her feel angry.

She took Charlotte back to the kitchen and made her some breakfast, as she ate her breakfast Jana made the calls to Rachel and Louise. 'Goodness Jana, you have had us all worried sick, where have you been' Rachel said anxiously.

'I'm so sorry to have worried you like that Rachel, I've lost all sense of time, I'm afraid.'

'What do you mean?' Jana went onto to explain to her about Charlotte and Brandon and how he had employed her to look after the child, she went on to tell her all about the nanny and what she had done to Charlotte. 'You remember Rachel, the little girl and her father we met down by the shops.' There was a pause before Rachel replied

'Ah…, yes I remember the little girl in the wheelchair and her handsome father, sorry Jana I think I have a hazy brain; the baby is leaving me without thought' Rachel said, and they both burst out laughing. They continued the conversation laughing and joking like old times, and before hanging up the phone Jana gave her Brandon's house number. 'for emergency calls only mind you' Jana said knowing full well that Rachel would call anyway and that she did not need an excuse.

Chapter Eight:
Gift of a Heart

With the call ended she dialled another number, this time she spoke to Louise, she sounded less anxious about not hearing from Jana than Rachel had. They chatted for some time; it was not as pleasant a chat like she had with Rachel. Louise talked about George telling her all about his funeral and how she still dearly missed him. 'Oh, I wish you were here Jana, I miss you so much.'

'I'll get back as soon as I can, Louise'

'Good' Louise said, sounding a little brighter. Jana gave her the same phone number that she provided Rachel before ending the call. Jana made her way back to the kitchen, where she had left Charlotte eating her breakfast.

'What took you so long?' Charlotte said cheekily.

'I was speaking to some of my friends on the phone' Jana said with a smile.

Jana took the empty dish away from in front of Charlotte, and she put it in the sink, she was about to fill it with soapy water to wash it when her phone rang. Answering the phone, Jana was puzzled to hear a man's voice on the other side. 'Hi Jana, it's me, Clive.'

'Clive who?'

'Clive Singleton, Shirley and Treavor's son.'

'Oh, I am so sorry Clive I did not recognise your voice, how can I help you?' Jana said

'I am sorry to be the bearer of bad news Jana, but I'm afraid my mother is no longer able to stay at your property.' Clive went onto explain, that his mother had been diagnosed a while back with dementia, and now it was so bad, she needed to go into a nursing home for twenty-four-hour care. 'I am so sorry to hear that Clive, please give your mother my best, thank you for letting me know'. Jana said with a heavy heart.

Jana had liked Mr and Mrs Singleton; she had spent many an hour in their company along with her grandparents. An arrangement was made for Jana to pick up the keys from a neighbour, Clive told her that he had dealt with his parent's belongings and that he had cleaned the house from top to bottom,

'It is ready for your next tenant to move in.'

'Thank you, Clive, you needn't have done all that' Jana said. Jana needed to get back home she needed to deal with the situation of finding a new tenant as soon as she could, she did not like the idea of the property being left empty for long. Brandon needed to be contacted, he needed to come home and watch his daughter. Jana went to find Brandon's number in his study. She took charlotte into the garden and gave her a book to read, while she looked for the telephone number. Jana searched through the rotary card file that was on his desk, it had been left open, and immediately she recognised the name on the card.

The name belonged to the private investigator Richard Wilson; Jana jotted down his number, but first, she needed to contact Brandon. Before she had a chance to call him the study phone rang. Jana answered the phone and waited for the caller to speak first, 'Hello Mr Black is that you?' the caller said 'Mr Black, it's Richard Wilson, I have the information you wanted on Miss Heart' he continued; Jana noticed a tremor in his voice, but this did not stop her from shouting at him down the phone. 'Mr Wilson, this is Jana Heart, please tell me what information you have on me and who is Mr Black? Jana said. Silence… Jana could not believe that Richard Wilson had put the phone down on her. She found the office number and dialled, the phone rang out for a while then a woman answered the phone, 'Brandon Blacks office how can I help you?'

Jana could feel her throat tightening, she could not answer the woman and slammed the phone receiver down into its cradle. She became a little dazed as she realised who Brandon was. Jana felt deceived again, as she realised what the connection was between Brandon and the private investigator. *"How long has he known who I am? When was he going to tell me who he is?"* Jana's mind was running away with her as these thoughts came one after each other. She needed answers and was determined to find out everything. Jana could not believe she had been so naïve, *"Why didn't I ask Richard Wilson his name, when he kept referring to him as Callum's brother?"* she began to torment herself, the very man she had been avoiding and having contact with him, the same man she has been employed by and was now living in his home with him for the last month. Jana paced the floor worryingly, back and forth, thinking about what she should do next. Making her mind up, Jana picked up the phone and redialled the number. The same woman answered the phone, Jana asked to speak to Brandon. 'Can I ask who's calling, please?' she asked.

Jana introduced herself to the receptionist, and the woman's tone changed, she was not as friendly as she had been when she answered the phone the first time. 'I'll put you through now' she said to Jana rudely. Jana waited as the line went quiet for a few seconds before Brandon came on the line. 'Jana is everything alright?' Brandon said with concern in his voice. It was Jana's turn to be silent, she could not forget how he had left his daughter like that, without speaking to her first and letting her know he would have to go to work. Brandon waited patiently on the other side before the silence was broken. Jana explained that she needed to get back to Britain as a matter of urgency and asked him to come back home for Charlotte. Brandon asked her to be patient as he needed to organise things and promised that he would ring her straight back, having no intentions of going back to the house. Brandon had not been able to sleep when he arrived at the apartment, all he could think about since leaving the house was Jana and how much she had come to mean to him in such a short time.

Brandon did not believe he would ever be able to let her go if he saw her again. *"It's better, that she goes back home, better for everyone concerned,"* he thought. Brandon called Jana back and explained that he was unable to leave, making an excuse about there being difficulties as work. He told her that he had contacted Charles and Martha. 'They won't be able to get a flight from England until tomorrow I'm afraid will you be able to stay until they arrive please?' She agreed to stay with Charlotte. 'Thank you, Jana, they will be arriving at the airport shortly after midnight, is that alright?' he asked. Jana did not answer the question directly and thanked him before hanging up the phone. Jana had only been with them a little over a month but felt unhappy that she was leaving, Jana knew she would miss Charlotte and had not had the chance to do any of the hydrotherapy exercises with Charlotte that she thought the little girl would benefit from. Jana wrote a letter to Brandon, reminding him of the type of physical exercise charlotte would need to be doing, and the type of qualified people that he would need to help Charlotte with them, the note was written and placed on his desk.

Jana went to get Charlotte, there was a lot of explaining to be done, Jana was going home and needed to explain to her why. A task she knew would be both heart-breaking for them both. Jana asked Charlotte if there was anything that she would like to do, eagerly Charlotte said that she would like to go to the beach and maybe go to one of the cafes for a cake. Jana agreed that they could do that and watched as the smile on Charlotte's face widened. Jana felt heavy-hearted, she knew she would be upsetting the child when she told her of her plans, they had both become very fond of each other during their short time together.

Jana called on her angel if there was any time that she needed divine guidance; this was the time. 'How am I going to find the right words to tell her I'm leaving' she asked the angel

'You will need to be ever so gentle little one, the child has had many losses in her young life which she blames herself for.' said the angel.

'What do you mean blames herself?'

'You will know soon enough; you must tell her you will be returning' the angel said

'I have no plans to return.'

'You will be returning little one' said the angel as it faded out and disappeared.

Jana silently thanked her angel for the support and love she had been receiving. In her own mind, however, Jana was determined not to return to Lanzarote. She booked a taxi to take them to the beach, she was unsure of the way and felt safer having a local driver take them. Jana telephoned a number that she found online for a local taxi firm who provided vehicles for the disabled and attempted to explain where she wanted to go. The difficulty between the language barrier became too much for the lady on the other end of the phone, and there was a pause before a male voice came on the line. The man could speak a little English, and with persistence from both parties and Jana spelling out the name of the beach, they were able to get a positive result. The taxi arrived at the door, Jana watched as the man securely fastened Charlotte and her wheelchair down with straps, making sure that the chair was unable to move around loosely.

The driver smiled at Jana and opened the front door for her to get inside, he chatted away in broken English. Jana realised it was the same man that she had spoken to on the telephone. Throughout the journey, she watched as he checked his rear-view mirror, frequently making sure that Charlotte was safe. The trip went relatively quiet, with the driver occasionally pointing out landmarks to them. They arrived at the beach a short while later, the driver unstrapped Charlotte and got her out of the taxi, with this duty completed he handed Jana a business card. 'Please ask for me, my name is Alejandro, and I will pick you up when you are ready.'

'Thank you, I will' said Jana as she handed him the fare for the ride. With a smile, Alejandro was gone, and they were left to their own devices. Jana pushed the wheelchair down the street towards the beach. There was a lot of people around, Jana watched as Charlotte tried to stretch around people's legs to look at what was happening. 'I'm sorry Charlotte there does not seem to be any gaps I can get you into for you to see what's going on.'

'What's happening?'

'I think there is a windsurfing competition happening' said Jana.

A voice came from behind, 'Jana, Jana...' as she turned, she could see it was Carlos, he was waving frantically at her as he came bounding towards them. 'whew... I did not think you would hear me with all this noise' he said

'Hello Carlos, what are you doing here? 'said Jana. They both heard a woman calling out to Carlos and turned to the direction the sound was coming from. A slim woman with brunette hair walked towards them she had two little boys running up close behind her. 'I am so sorry, my love, please let me do the introductions'' Carlos said, speaking to the woman.'

'Jana, please meet my wife Katie and my sons Andres and Alberto'

Jana shook Katie's hand and said hi to the boys,

'This little lady is Charlotte' Jana said.

Charlotte smiled and said hello in a whisper of a voice, Jana had not seen her so shy before. 'How are you enjoying the windsurfing?' Katie asked.

'Not so good, Charlotte can't see around the people' said Jana.

Carlos smiled at Charlotte and handed the bag he was holding to his wife, he bent down and picked charlotte up out of her chair and lifting her on his shoulders, asked what she could see. Jana could see Charlotte smile and her eyes widen as she took in the scene. 'Well?' Carlos asked. Charlotte went onto describe the windsurfers and their boards.

'There are lots of men and women on the wind things' said Charlotte.

'They are windsurfing boards, what do they look like?' Carlos asked as he heard the excitement in her voice.

'They look like surfboards, but they all have a big sail. 'Why do they have sails?' Charlotte said in a puzzled tone.

'so that the wind can take them at speed' said Carlos. Carlos stood there for a while with Charlotte on his shoulders watching the race, the boys went forward into the crowd to see for themselves, 'Don't go too far boys stay as close as you can to your father' Katie shouted to them. Katie asked Jana if she would like to help her get some ice-creams and the women left them to watch the race.

On the way back the women saw that the boys had returned and Carlos had put Charlotte back in her chair, the children were chattering to each other as they walked towards them, the boys turning to see that they had ice-cream ran towards their mother to get theirs. Alberto handed Charlotte her ice-cream, and the boys sat back, where they had previously been sitting, right next to Charlotte's chair. The three adults sat on the bench and listened as the children laughed and chatted. The boys were asking Charlotte why she was in a wheelchair when she told them that she was in an accident they, shrugged their shoulders in innocence and carried on chatting. The afternoon went by, and time had flown; they were all having so much fun. They did not realise the time, and it was almost five o'clock, after saying their goodbyes, Carlos and his family went home. Jana and charlotte headed to the café for Charlotte to have the pastry that she had been promised. Jana did not realise that she was so hungry until she could smell the food as they entered the café.

Looking over the menu she decided to have a vegetable paella, and Charlotte asked for a pizza, drinks were ordered and arrived at the table soon after. Jana chatted to charlotte telling her about her plans to go back to Britain.

'Do you have to go?'

'I'm afraid, so yes, it is important' said Jana.

'When will you be back?' Charlotte asked.

'To be honest, I don't know' Jana said.

Their meal arrived, and they ate in in silence, Jana knew that she had upset Charlotte and wished with all her heart it could have been so different. They decided to take their cakes home to eat later, none of them really had an appetite anymore and had only managed to eat a small part of their meal. Jana called the taxi and asked for Alejandro to pick them up for their return fare. The taxicab arrived ten minutes after and with Charlotte safely strapped into the car, they headed back to the house. Charlotte never uttered a word on the way back to the house, Jana tried to make conversation with her without success. She had a distressed look on her face the entire journey back.

They arrived back at the house to Martha greeting them. 'When did you get back?' Jana asked. 'I managed to get a seat on the flight this morning, Charles will be coming tomorrow. I understand you need to get home urgently' Martha said

'Yes, yes I do' Jana said.

' Come on buttercup let's get you in the shower and to bed' Martha said to Charlotte bending down to kiss the top of her head, neither of the two women had seen the tears streaming down Charlotte's face, she held her head down and Martha had taken this as a sign she was tired. Jana watched as she was wheeled away, her heart beating hard against her chest, Jana knew that she would need to leave as soon as she could, or it would be too difficult for her to go. Firstly, she would need to speak to Louise, she rang her number, and the phone was picked up almost immediately.

'Hello, Louise.'

Jana, are you alright?' Louise asked, concerned as she could almost sense the tears running down Jana's face. 'I have a favour to ask of you' said Jana.

Jana told her what had happened and how she needed to go back home to get new tenants in place. Holding her breath, she asked Louise if she could stay with her so that she could check any future tenants. Jana knew that Louise lived quite a distance from her cottage but thought that a train back home would be comfortable enough from Louise's. 'of course, you can, there really is no need to ask.' Jana thanked Louise and hung up the phone, Jana would have to go and pack. She needed to think about booking a flight for the morning. Jana headed to her room to complete the daunting task. Jana was passing Charlotte's bedroom when she heard the child crying. In-between the sobbing, she could hear her talking to her grandmother.

'Why does she have to go?'

'I don't know my darling, maybe she has work to go to' said Charlotte's grandmother.

'I don't want her to go, is it my fault, did I do something again?' Charlotte said as she sobbed into her grandmothers' shoulder. 'Hush child' her grandmother said as she rocked her back and forth, it was not long before Charlotte had cried herself to sleep.

Jana could feel the tears running down her own cheeks as she went into her room. She lay on her bed, her heart-breaking, she did not want to hurt Charlotte. She would make sure that Charlotte knew it was not her fault, even if it meant that she had to tell her the truth. Jana drifted off into a deep sleep. She was in the dark street again, the glow of the lights more menacing than ever before, Jana looked up the road to see a familiar scene. Two men were shoving another man into the car at gunpoint, Jana screamed as the man in the car turned to look at her, she could see his face. It was Justin… Jana was tossing and turning as the faceless man had grabbed her again, demanding to know where his property was, he was spitting in her face as he shouted. Jana knew it was just a dream but could not stop herself from shaking, she could not come away from the nightmare.

Jana was screaming now calling her angel to help, she began to feel a warmth around her, the scene was fading into the background, she opened her eyes to see her angel standing there. There was a glow around the angel, a shining, a different radiance to what she had seen before. Jana felt the warmth envelope her and hearing soothing music, never having listened to anything so beautiful it was like the angels were singing… soon she was calm and drifted back off to sleep. The daylight shone through the windows waking Jana; Jana looked at the clock on her bedside cabinet, it was five-thirty. Remembering that she had not packed her case or booked her flight, she hurried to take a shower. The shower was a release from the stickiness of her body, Jana remembered the dream vividly and the trapped feeling she had experienced. Jana sent a silent thank you up to her angel for helping her.

The house was silent as she made her way down the stairs, she could hear someone pottering around in the kitchen as she entered it. 'Morning Jana' said Martha.

'Morning, what are you doing up so early?' Jana said. Martha was quiet and did not answer for a while.

'I slept in the chair next to charlottes bed' Martha said as she turned to face Jana.

'Is Charlotte alright?' Jana said as she watched for tell-tale signs on Martha's face. Martha had difficulty hiding her expression, she could not hide anything.

'To be honest Jana, I don't think that she is,

'Why what's wrong' said Jana.

'Charlotte is blaming herself for you leaving today, she thinks she has done something wrong.' Martha said with sadness in her eyes. Jana explained that she had heard them both chatting away as she came to bed, and how she had heard Charlotte crying, and her telling Martha that it was her fault again. 'What did she mean again?' Jana said asking her about the remark that Charlotte had made. Martha went quiet and turned away to look out of the window, Jana knew she was crying and went over to comfort her. As she got closer, Martha held her hand up to stop her.

Taking a deep breath, she explained to Jana that Charlotte was blaming herself for the death of her mother and grandparents. 'Charlotte was playing up a bit in the car, demanding to stop for a drink' Martha said.

'Oh, poor thing 'said Jana.

'Well, she could be a right little madam in those days, to be honest, she was spoiled rotten and got most of her own way.'

'She is not like that now' said Jana.

'No, she is far from the child that she was. Now when something happens, like your leaving, she blames herself.' said Martha. Jana reassured Martha that she would get Charlotte to believe her when she tells her it was not her fault.

Jana promised that she would explain things openly and honestly to them both after Charlotte got out of bed and had her breakfast. 'Are you alright?' Martha asked Jana. Remembering that she had heard Jana screaming, she explained that she was about to come into her room to see what was happening. Then it went quiet, 'I opened the door a little and saw that you were sleeping peacefully, I reassured myself that you were alright before I left.'

'Just one of those nightmares again.' Jana said.

'They say that if you remember your dreams as vivid as you do, that they are messages and not simply dreams' said Martha.

'No, I did not know that' Jana said with a worried look on her face.

'What is it, Jana? What is worrying you? Please talk to me, let me help' said Martha.

'I saw someone I know in my dream; someone I knew very well in my past.' Jana said.

Changing the subject, Jana asked Martha if they could go into the garden with their coffee *"It's such a beautiful day it would be a shame to waste it"* Jana thought to herself. They chatted about mundane topics while they waited for Charlotte to wake.

It was a warm morning, and Martha had left her window open. Martha knew that they would be able to hear Charlotte from where they were sitting. As they chatted, they watched as the birds flew from tree to tree, listening to them singing their morning songs, enjoying the peace and quiet, both left to their own thoughts. Jana was thinking about how she was going to tell Charlotte how she could say the truth to the child without further hurting her. Martha was thinking what a fool Brandon was for letting this young girl walk out of his life. The silence between the two women was accepted with there being only fleeting glances between them. Jana began to speak first.

'Have you noticed charlotte talking in her room when she is alone? she asked.

'Yes, quite often, why do you ask?'

'I have heard and seen her talking, sometimes she gets very distressed.'

'She tells us that she is speaking to Lucy. She is my daughter and Charlotte's mother' Martha said.

'Can I ask, do any of you believe her?'

'My husband is a little sceptical and Brandon is in full denial, but yes, yes I do. Why do you ask Jana, do you think something is wrong?' Martha asked with concern.

Jana was afraid to tell her about her own abilities to talk to spirit for fear that Martha may think she was insane. Jana touched her angel pin, she had worn it this morning automatically, not thinking about it. Within a blink of an eye, Lucy appeared, *"Where is my angel?"* Jana thought, looking around. Lucy smiled at her, 'don't be afraid to tell my mother, she understands more than you know' Lucy said.

'What is it, Jana? Martha asked. She had seen Jana looking to her right with a puzzled look on her face.

'I will explain everything to you, but first, you must promise me that you will not say anything to Brandon.' Martha promised Jana that she would not say anything as she began to cross her fingers under the table.

Jana told Martha about the accident, and when the angel had first appeared to her. Jana explained how she was now able to see and speak to the spirit and how she had her own near-death experience, and it was then that she was told it was now her mission to help others, both in the spirit world and on the earth. 'Please don't think me insane, Martha.'

'I don't, and I won't. I have been to many mediums in my lifetime, my daughter also believed in the spirit world and always said that she would come back someday. I truly believe she has and that Charlotte talks to her' Martha said.

'Yes, she does, she has most nights that I have been here.' Jana said. Martha was about to ask Jana some questions when they heard charlotte calling. Martha went to get Charlotte and Jana prepared some breakfast. Charlotte was smiling as she came into the kitchen, Martha placed her by the table, and Jana put her breakfast in front of her. 'Excuse me, I just have to go and get something' Jana said before she dashed out of the room.

It was not long, and Jana was back, she heard Charlotte chatting away to her grandmother. As Jana sat down, Charlotte held her hand out and opened her palm, inside she had a friendship bracelet. 'Mummy told me to give you this, she said you will always remember me and that you will return to us one day' Charlotte said.

'Thank you, Charlotte' Jana said, giving her a hug. She was not going to make a promise that she will return to her, she could not make that promise. Jana put her hand in her pocket and pulled out a little jewellery box, containing a heart shaped necklace made from sea glass, handing the box over to Charlotte she watched as the child's eyes opened wide and the smile reached the tops of her cheeks. 'Thank you, Jana'

'It's not from me, it is a special gift with a special message' said Jana

'What's the message?' Charlotte asked eagerly.

'The gift is from your mother, and she would like her little snowdrop to know that it was not and will never be your fault that she died' Jana said. Both Jana and Charlotte looked up to see that Lucy was standing in front of them.

Jana told Martha that Lucy was there, Martha could not see her, but she knew from the look on her granddaughter's face that she could see her. 'You will find out in time who is to blame Charlotte, remember that I love you and it is not your fault. I have to go now snowdrop, for a little while' Lucy said as she faded into nothingness.

'Mummy is so pretty, isn't she' Charlotte said looking at her grandmother.

'Yes, my darling she is beautiful' Martha answered with tears streaming down her face. Martha mouthed the words is silence 'Thank you,' Jana nodded her head in response. They left Charlotte to eat her breakfast and went back out into the garden out of earshot. Martha thanked Jana for following her out, she had not wanted to ask her directly, she had silently tilted her head slightly a couple of times to indicate that is what she wanted her to do. Out in the Garden Martha made Jana promise that she would not tell Brandon that his daughter was seeing her mother. Martha then said to Jana that Brandon believed that Charlotte was having dreams because she still misses her mother and continues to grieve for her. Martha was fearful that if he were to find out, he would take her to a therapist.

Jana was horrified at this… 'Would he not believe his child? 'Jana asked as she took in the difficulty that Charlotte must have to hide what she was seeing. 'No, he thinks that it is all rubbish and that people are just out to scam innocent and grieving people' Martha said. Jana promised not to tell him about Charlotte, *"I shall have to speak to Charlotte about this myself, poor little thing may be finding it difficult to understand, I know I am" Jana* thought. Charlotte was calling again, Martha went to attend to her, and Jana went up to her room to think, she understood what the child was going through and needed to find out how she could help her in the best way possible. As she walked into her room Jana saw her suitcase on the bed, she had forgotten she was in the process of packing and yet to book her flight home.

Jana called the airline the only flight available to her was to Manchester airport at ten-fifty in the morning. She would have to ask Martha if she could stay another night, she would get a taxi to take her to the airport in the morning. She went down to speak to Martha, who was more than happy she would be staying. Jana hugged her and went back up to her room. The flight booked, she finished her packing and called Louise. Jana told Louise that she would be landing at approximately three o'clock in the afternoon.

'I should arrive at your house at about six in the evening.'

'Why so long?' Said Louise.

'I will be getting a bus from the airport; it always takes longer that way' Jana said.

'No-no, myself and Joe will come and pick you up' said Louise.

Jana had tried to protest, but Louise was having none of it. Jana did not want to feel that she put on anyone, it seemed she did not have much choice. She had not driven since the accident, and with the loss of her arm, she had lost all confidence in herself.

Jana went down to see Charlotte, she wanted to get her into the pool so that she could show her some exercises that she wanted her to do until her father could arrange for someone to help her. Charlotte beamed when Jana explained that she would be there another night. 'Oh, goody we can have a girly day' Charlotte said Laughing.

'Oh, no…' Martha said, putting her head in her hands as she teased Charlotte. Jana looked on puzzled, Charlotte and Martha both looked at her and began laughing. Martha explains that a girly day meant a day of mess and cleaning up afterwards 'Well… cleaning up for the adults that is 'she said.

'Yay, now we can make daddy a cake for when he comes home' Charlotte said excitedly.' It was the adults turn to laugh now. Jana agreed that she would join in on the messy proceedings of baking cakes, but only if Charlotte would do some exercises in the pool. Charlotte pulled a pouting face but was soon reminded by her grandmother that it was Charlie's golden rule number two.

Still pouting Charlotte reluctantly agreed to do as she was told. Martha took her to get ready, telling Jana they would meet her by the pool. Jana asked if Martha would join them as well, she still lacked confidence in herself and would appreciate the support. Martha smiled and nodded her head in understanding. The pool had been altered to make things easier for Charlotte, a ramp had been put into the shallow end of the indoor pool, and there was a specially designed type of wheelchair where she's able to come from the dressing room into the pool. Jana was in the pool when they arrived Martha pushed Charlotte down into the pool, it was evident to Jana that the little girl was still in fear of the water and what would happen to her. 'Come on, you are going to be fine' said Jana.

'What 's that in your hand and those things floating around you?' Charlotte said inquisitively.

'These are floats to help you keep your head above the water.'

'How?' asked Charlotte.

'Let me show you' Jana said.

Jana demonstrated how she wanted Charlotte to use the floats reassuring her that she would be safe and reminding her that both herself and Martha would be there to help her. Charlotte did as she was instructed, leaning over the floats with just her legs dangling down, Jana was able to bend her knees and manipulate the muscles with the appropriate exercise for them. Jana had kept a note pad over by the side of the pool to take notes, as she teased and tickled Charlotte, she observed that the child had feelings in her legs and feet. This puzzled Jana as she believed the child to have had spinal injuries which would prevent such feelings.

'Charlie, Charlie' they could hear someone calling.

'Daddy, daddy. I'm in here' Charlotte shouted back as they watched Brandon walk through the door. Brandon looked shocked to see Martha had arrived sooner than expected, he had not expected to see her there and wondered why Jana had not left yet. Jana had all the intentions of leaving before Brandon arrived and was just as shocked seeing him standing there. He excused himself and said he had some unfinished work to complete.

Charlotte was too excited to stay in the pool any longer she wanted to spend time with her father. It was almost lunchtime when they had finished dressing, Martha took Charlotte to Brandon and then joined Jana in the kitchen to prepare some lunch. It was while they were in the kitchen that Charles arrived. They could hear him chatting to Brandon and Charlotte in the study before he came into the kitchen and kissed his wife lovingly. Lunch was a light affair with sandwiches and cold drinks. They all chatted over lunch, Jana and Brandon kept their eyes averted from each other, with them looking fleetingly at each other on occasion. Brandon and Jana had not realised just how obvious they had been to the other adults around the table. Charles looked at Martha and shrugged, *"I am going to have to speak to that boy"* he thought to himself as he looked towards Brandon. Jana excused herself and left the table, she felt that she would begin to cry at any moment.

Jana realised how much more Brandon was coming to mean to her and did not think she would be able to hold the tears back much longer, she still felt angry at his deceit for not telling her who he really was. She ran to her room and lay on her bed, allowing the pressure out, *"Why am I feeling this way?"* She thought as the tears flowed down her cheeks. Martha had followed her; she was distressed to hear Jana cry so bitterly but thought better of disturbing her at this time. Martha joined Charles in the sitting room, she was telling him about Jana sobbing.

'I really don't know what to do Charles.'

'I know what to do, you will need to take Charlotte out, I don't want her to hear what I have to say to her father.' Said Charles angrily.

'I had better ask Jana to join us then' Martha said.

Martha took a cup of tea to Jana's room, where she found her asleep, she gently shook her awake. Jana came around in a bit of a daze, she had not intended to go to sleep, she sat up and took the tea off Martha thanking her as she did so. Martha explained that Charlotte needed new clothes and that they were going shopping. Martha asked if Jana would like to join them. She jumped at the chance; Jana did not relish the thought of bumping into Brandon. Martha left the room to let Jana dress, arranging to meet her a half-hour later by the front door.

Chapter Nine:
Angel on the Wing

Charles watched as they drove off down the drive. *"Right now, it's time to have a word with that son-in-law of mine,"* he thought. He found Brandon in his study working. 'If only you would take your mind off work occasionally Brandon you would be able to see what is right in front of your face.' Charles said as he let his frustration toward Brandon show. Brandon stared at his father-in-law, not quite believing what he was saying and how he was speaking to him. 'I'm sorry, is there a problem?' said Brandon trying to keep himself calm.

'Yes- yes, there is. I am sorry, but over the years I have watched you as you have let your daughter down and now, I have to watch it again.' Charles said, standing up straight, ready for the confrontation that he knew would come. Brandon stood up and came from around the desk, he was surprisingly calm. Charles did not know what to make of it.

Charles was expecting Brandon to fly off the handle and be angry at him. Instead, he stood in front of Charles and in a sobering manner and nodded as he spoke. 'Yes, Charles, I am aware that I have let my daughter down in the past. Please enlighten me as to how I am letting her down now.' Charles was taken aback by how Brandon had responded. It was not, however going to stop him getting everything off his mind. 'That child has lost her mother and grandparents she has gone through a lot of loss in her young years, don't you see that she is going to lose someone she loves again. Brandon, you are also going to lose someone that you feel deeply for.'

'Charles, what are you talking about?' Brandon said he was confused now what was Charles talking about.

'Jana, it is obvious to both Martha and I that you have feelings for this young lady. Why are you letting her walk away?'

'I am not letting her walk away. Jana has her own life; she needs to return to the UK, and I do not have any right to stop her, Charles' said Brandon.

Brandon was feeling embarrassed that his in-laws would notice he had feelings for another woman other than their daughter. 'Now please if you don't mind, I need to get back to work' Brandon said, leaving Charles to do nothing other than stare after his back as he walked away. Charles was still annoyed at Brandon and let him know so when joining him in the garden sometime later. Handing him a drink, Brandon admitted that he owed him an explanation, he asked Charles to remain patient, so he could explain what was happening. 'I really don't know how much you want to hear' Brandon said.

'Everything, I would like to know everything' said Charles.

'I think Jana may be the woman who saved Cullum's life' Brandon said as he continued to explain that he had asked a private investigator to find her as he wanted to thank her personally. 'What happened?' said Charles.

'She defiantly would not accept my thanks personally' Brandon said

'Does she know who you are?'

'No, I don't believe she does' Brandon said.

Charles looked at Brandon with sadness, could he not see what he was doing. 'You need to let things lie; Jana obviously has her reasons for not wanting a personal thank you from a stranger.' Charles said. Brandon wondered what he meant as a look of sadness came over Charles's face, he promised Charles that he would try and forget about it but admitted to it being painful. What he did not tell Charles was that he had the investigator looking into Jana's background. 'You cannot get everything your own way, Brandon. You can be quite forceful and demanding on time, and to be quite truthful, we are all feeling your wrath.

Do you think that is really fair?' Charles said, being frankly honest with him. Brandon did not respond, and they both sat there quietly thinking about what each other had said as they drank their drinks. Martha, Jana and Charlotte reached the shopping mall.

As they got out of the car, they could feel the heat, it was still quite warm. Taking charlotte out of the vehicle, Martha suggested that they go for a cold drink before they went shopping. They sat outside a small café with their juices, Charlotte asked if she could have a cookie. They watched as she crumbled the cookie onto her plate then wheeled herself towards some pigeons looking for food in front of the row of cafés. Charlotte fed the crumbs to the pigeons and began laughing as they all flew onto her trying to take the bits off the plate. Martha took the opportunity to speak to Jana while Charlotte was not able to hear them. She had been concerned that Jana had remained quiet throughout the journey. She asked if there was anything, she could do to help her. 'Yes, there is something I need help with' Jana said

'What is it, child?' Martha said

'I am going to stay at the hotel by the airport tonight, do you think Charles will take me there this evening?'

Of course, he will, but why do you want to stay there. You will have sufficient time to leave in the morning' Martha said curiously. Jana did not answer but simply smiled.

Martha knew when to stop asking questions and shouted out to Charlotte to come and finish her drink. They both looked at the child and smiled as Charlotte was still giggling when she got back to the table. Charlotte had decided that morning that she would choose her own clothes and reminded the two women of that in no uncertain terms that it was what she was going to do. 'I suppose you are going to pay for all your own clothes too little madam, are you?' Martha said

'No...' Charlotte said with a scared look on her face. Jana was unable to contain the laughter that was creeping up into her throat and began laughing so hard that the tears ran down her cheeks, and her ribs started hurting. Martha laughed as well, Charlotte did not find it funny and began to pout, her brows and lips coming in a downward movement as she did so, but this only made the women laugh harder. Holding onto her ribs, Jana stood up to go with Martha doing the same as they watched Charlotte wheel herself off, still annoyed at them.

Back at the house, Charles had taken himself off for a nap. Brandon remained in the garden thinking about what Charles had said, *"He was right; she must have a good reason why she does not want me to thank her personally"* he thought. Brandon promised himself to speak to Jana and let her know that he was Callum's brother before she went back to the UK. *"How am I going to tell her? It will have to be in a gentle way" he thought.* He sat there for a while until the phone started ringing and broke his chain of thoughts. Brandon answered the phone, it was Richard Wilson, he told him that he had sent through the background documentation for Jana via email, Richard could not pluck up the courage to say to him about the phone call with Jana and her questioning him about the information that he was asked to find on her. Brandon thanked him and said his payment would be in his bank account in the morning. Richard hung up the phone without responding to Brandon, he was relieved that he had not been questioned about the call, he realised that Brandon Black had no idea that Jana had spoken to him.

Brandon sat staring at the computer, something like this would have him looking at it immediately. He did not know why but felt that he did not want to know what was in the report and could not make up his mind as to whether to open the document or not. The decision was taken from him as he heard his daughter shouting out to him. 'I'm in here Charlie' he said

'I have a new shirt for you, Jana helped me to pick it out' Charlotte said excitedly

'Where is Jana? Brandon said, looking over her shoulder.

'She's gone' Martha said from the doorway.

'What do you mean gone?'

'She's staying at the airport hotel tonight, ready for her flight home tomorrow 'Martha said as she saw the look of anger reach his eyes, oh he knew well how to hide his fury from Charlotte. but he was not so good at hiding it from the adults.

The journey to the airport was dragging for Jana, she liked Charles but wanted to be on her own. Charles glanced over a couple of times and caught her wiping away tears. Jana was looking out of the window and trying her best not to let him see how hurt she was. He did not question Jana but handed her a handkerchief, he could not sit there, making Jana believe that there was no one there for her. As they arrived at the hotel, Jana asked Charles to drop her off at the front of the hotel, she did not want his sympathy. Pulling up outside, Charles got out of the car and walked around to the passenger side, he was not going to let her walk away from him without a goodbye because of his stubborn son-in-law. Hugging her, he kissed her on the cheek, there was no need for words and Jana hugged him just as hard as he hugged her. All alone in the hotel room, Jana could let the tears flow freely. She had become so fond of the family in such a short time and leaving them was breaking her heart. *"What am I going to do now, why can't I just be happy? Help me please"* she thought as she cried bitterly.

Jana began to relax as she could feel it, the gentleness and warmth of her angel's wings around her. She could not see her angel, but she could feel its presence and hear the words *"everything will be alright little one"* whispered gently in her ear. It was not long before Jana was calm again, no longer wanting to be on her own Jana decided to go and have a drink in the bar. It was not often that she had alcohol when she was upset, but Jana felt the need for one now. At the bar she ordered herself a vodka and orange with ice, as she sipped it, she felt the cold ease her throat, she had been crying so hard her throat had become a little sore. Jana ordered another drink and this time took it to a table overlooking the window. As she looked out of the window, Jana wondered what Brandon was doing, she doubted if he even missed her just a little.

At the house Brandon was consoling his daughter, Martha and Charles looking on glanced a knowing look at each other. They both knew that Jana's leaving would have a negative influence on Charlotte, on Brandon too, only he was too stubborn to notice. Leaving him to console his daughter, they went down to the kitchen. Martha was making some tea when her husband started speaking to her in an angry voice, not towards her it was her son-in-law that he was mad at, 'I don't know what the hell is wrong with Brandon, I'm sure he's wearing blinkers. I know that he can't see what's before him' Charles said.

'did you speak to him this afternoon Charles.'

'yes, to be honest, he just skirted around the issue, telling me I was right but not admitting to himself that he was wrong' Charles said.

'Oh well, we will just have to let him find out the hard way himself. There is no more we can do other than be there supporting our granddaughter Charles.' Martha said sternly.

Charles nodded his head in response, Martha knew better, Charles could be just as stubborn as Brandon.

None of them had heard Brandon coming downstairs and going into his study. He sat at the computer looking at his emails, his finger hovering over the email Richard Wilson had sent him. Brandon had thought about opening it a few times throughout the day and was either distracted or could not pull himself together to open it. Brandon sat there confused, he did not know why he was not opening it, he had never had problems like this before. He felt the need to clear his head and decided to take a swim, something Brandon often did when trying to solve a problem, just as he was about to leave the room the phone rang.

'Brandon you need to come as soon as you can, I've sent the chopper to come and get you. It should be there in fifteen minutes.' Brandon's secretary was frantically telling him over the phone.

'Calm down, Kirsty, what is going on?' Brandon said to his extremely anxious secretary.

'There has been a serious incident, you have to come right away' she said, hanging up the phone. Brandon went to find Martha and Charles. He needed to explain what had happened and ask them to look after his daughter while he was away.

Before leaving, he wanted to see Charlotte, he wanted to say goodbye to her, he found her sleeping fast. Brandon kissed her on the forehead and asked Martha to explain to her what had happened in the morning. He could hear the helicopter, and throwing some things into a bag quickly, he kissed Martha on the cheek and thanked her before running out of the door and getting into the chopper. Martha and Charles watched as the helicopter took off into the air, Brandon waving at them as it did so. 'I wonder what that is about' said Charles.

'He will let us know soon enough.' Martha said as she shut the door, shutting the night out. 'Time for bed I think' Charles said. Martha nodded and yawned at the same time; they were both getting sleepy and would need all their strength to deal with Charlotte in the morning.

Jana was asleep in the hotel room, she was dreaming again, but this was not the same dream. In this dream, Brandon was holding her, gently caressing her face running his hands down her arms. He grabbed her waist and held onto it tightly but gently, Jana could feel a shudder go through her as she took a sharp intake of breath. They were dancing, and Jana looked to see if anyone was watching them, the room was empty; there was only the two of them in there. Brandon spun her around the large ballroom, spinning and spinning until she felt dizzy. She looked again; now they were in a large bedroom, Brandon continued to hold her waist as he lifted her onto the bed. Leaning over her, he began to caress her face, holding it in one of his large hands. Brandon leaned forward to kiss her, his other hand moving over her throbbing breast.

Jana could hear bells ringing; she was awakened by the alarm going off. She sat on the edge of the bed for some time, dazed and confused; the dream had seemed so real it had been like Brandon had been right there with her. Jana did not know whether to laugh or cry, feelings of the elation and the gentleness of his touch as they were about to make love remained with her. She could also feel the loneliness and sadness that morning had brought, Jana missed Brandon very much and wanted to feel his arms around her for real and not just in a dream. She shook the thoughts out of her head, she needed to get ready to go to the airport. Her bags were packed, Jana waited outside the main entrance for the taxi to take her to the terminal building. During her journey to the airport, Jana was beginning to feel uncomfortable; she was getting a similar feeling that something terrible was going to happen, Jana still had a long way to go before she fully understood where the senses would guide her.

Arriving at the airport Jana booked in and headed for the security, she felt uncomfortable when people rushed to get through there and needed to have it behind her. Going through the security, Jana showed them the letter that was carried in her bag explaining about her prosthetic arm, once through, she went to purchase something to read on the flight. The headlines in the newspapers caught her eye, a ship had caught fire in the Caribbean, there had been a massive rescue operation done during the night, and some of the passengers had been taken to hospital with smoke inhalation; fortunately, there had been no fatalities. *"Poor things,"* Jana thought to herself and sent a prayer of help for those on the cruise to the angels. The announcement came for them to board the plane and she stood in the queue waiting to board when a second announcement came over the loudspeaker that the aircraft was now delayed for an hour. Sighing Jana went to find a seat to wait and watched as others complained and moaned at the airline staff. *"What is the use of arguing with them, there is no point. There is nothing the staff can do."* Jana thought.

Jana telephoned Louise to tell her about the delay and apologise for it. 'Don't be silly; it's not your fault, these things happen.'

'I know, but I don't like putting you out.'

'You're not putting us out Jana, we are keeping track of the flight. Are you alright?' Louise asked her as she could hear the sadness in Jana's voice.

'I am fine, I'm just a little tired, and missing charlotte already that's all' Jana said before saying goodbye and hanging up the phone. She watched the people around her, Jana liked to people watch and try and guess their occupation. It helped her take her mind off her own thoughts, this time, it didn't help. A crowd was gathering over by the window, Jana went to see what was happening and looking down at the plane could see an ambulance had pulled up. Jana knew it was not good news she had been having the prickly feelings throughout the morning, the same feelings she gets when there is death about to happen around her. Jana wished the individuals soul a safe journey back home, before sitting back down.

Jana's memories went back to the deaths of her own relatives when she was at a young age and the different feelings that she had experienced then. She remembered the emotions as if it were yesterday. How she had been left to feel abandoned, isolated and alone, which was how she was feeling now. Her thoughts were distracted by a woman sitting next to her, 'Are you ok, you're looking quite pale' she said to Jana.

'Yes, thank you. I am fine.' Jana said, smiling. The woman turned back to reading her book, Jana looked on at the people around her, *"this is a long hour"* she thought as she checked the time on her watch, she just wanted to be home now. It was some time before the announcement came that the plane was ready. People rushed to get to the front of the queue, Jana marvelled at how they resembled sheep following each other, pushing and shoving to get to the front. She remained in her seat until everyone else was on board, *"the plane can't leave without me."* She thought; chuckling to herself.

Once seated on the plane, Jana knew that it was going to be a long journey. The flight home was going to take at least four hours and fifteen minutes, and a small child was sitting next to her who was already becoming upset by the sound of the engines. The plane started to move on the tarmac below. Jana prepared herself, she did not enjoy the taking off and landings because they made her feel uncomfortable. The little girl next to her could not have been more than three years old, and she began to cry. Jana could see the fear in the child's face, and before she knew it, she was talking to the child reassuring her that everything was going to be alright. 'Look, there is an angel on the wing, looking after us' Jana said. The little girl looked out of the window and stopped crying, she began to wave, this time, Jana could not see what she was waving at, and neither could the child's mother. As the plane levelled out, the child tried to climb out of her seatbelt, her mother undid the belt, and immediately the child climbed onto Jana's lap.

The little girl stared out of the window, smiling and saying 'Look mummy look' pulling at her mothers' arm. 'I am so sorry about this; I'm Katie, and this little rascal is Lizzie,' she said, introducing them. 'Hi, I'm Jana, there is absolutely no problem, Lizzie is welcome to share my seat and watch the clouds go by' Jana said

'No.., angels' Lizzie said, putting her little hand on Jana's cheek and pushing it so that she was looking out of the window.

'Oh, I am so sorry, Lizzie.' said Jana, smiling. The adults continued to chat as Lizzie watched out of the window. Katie thanked Jana again for allowing her daughter to sit with her, it's usually a nightmare when we fly, Lizzie often cries for the longest part of the journey, I have never seen her so quiet and so preoccupied. Lizzie was tapping on Jana's hand she had not noticed that the tapping was making a noise on her arm, she just continued to stare out of the window smiling. Jana was just grateful for the distraction; Jana could not stop thinking about Brandon, and the pain was becoming unbearable. Lizzie began to feel a little too heavy for Jana to hold, when she looked down, she found the child sleeping. Katie removed Lizzie from Jana's lap and lay her on the seat between them, as she did so, a man not much older than Katie stood in the aisle by the side of her. He was looking down and smiling. The man looked at Jana and realised that she could see him, his smile widened as he said, 'Please tell my sister and niece that I love them very much.' Jana nodded and watched as he looked down at them again.

Jana had not noticed the sadness in Katie's eye's until now, she looked back at the man and speaking through her mind she asked his name and how he had died, explaining to him that she would need as much information as possible to tell his sister. He told her his name was Glen and that he had been killed while Skiing. He had slipped, and his neck had snapped as he rolled down the mountainside. 'Please tell her 'I passed quickly and that I was not in pain'. He went on to say that his sister was travelling back home to go to his funeral.

This was the first time Jana had been given anything for a stranger, and she knew she would have to proceed carefully. 'Katie, please don't think me crazy, I have a message for you from the spirit world' Jana said

'What do you mean?' Katie said, looking puzzled.

'Your brother Glen is here with you, and he wants me to pass a message on for him, is that alright' said Jana

'Please do' Katie said not really knowing whether to believe Jana or not.

'Glen asked me to tell you that when he had his skiing accident, he went quickly and was not in pain. He also tells me that you are travelling back to go to his funeral.' Jana looked at Glen who was now rapidly trying to pass on more messages, 'he would also like me to tell you that he has a will and that it is with his solicitor, you will find the details of his solicitor and his insurance documents in his safe at the office.'

Jana went onto tell her how much he loved her and Lizzie and how he regrets not having the chance to see them before he died. Katie had been crying throughout, Jana tried to reassure her that she was not out to upset her, she was only passing on the message. Katie knew that there was no way that Jana had been able to know any of the information. She explained to Jana that Glen had been the last of her remaining family and that it was just her and her daughter left now. Jana could not continue; the plane began to jolt as it hit turbulent weather, the captain came over the loudspeaker asking the passengers to put on their safety belts. Katie hurried to wake Lizzie and put her seatbelt on her before fastening her own. People began to scream as the turbulence got worse, Lizzie began to cry. It was then that Jana's own angel stood in the aisle, the radiance of the angel had a calming effect over all the children on the plane and Jana watched as she saw Lizzie look up into her angel's face and smile.

Lizzie turned to look at Jana and innocently said 'Celeste.' As she pointed at the angel, Jana's angel smiled and nodded. The plane stopped juddering, and a calmness came over everyone. 'I hate when that happens' said Katie, everything else forgotten for the time being. 'Thirty minutes before we land in Manchester, would all cabin crew prepare for landing' the captain was announcing. You could hear the sigh of relief from some of the passengers and Jana herself gave an inner sigh of relief. She needed to feel safe and secure and not just because of the flight, she needed to get back to normality as quickly as she could. It was forty-five minutes before Jana was walking through the arrivals area after picking up her suitcase, whenever Jana went away, her bag always seemed to be one of the last to come off the carousel. As she walked through, she could see Louise frantically waving and shouting her name.

The two women hugged for such a time Joe thought he would have to prize them apart. 'Get a move on ladies, let's go and beat the traffic' he said as he hugged Jana. Taking Jana's suitcase away from her, he led the way back to the car. Inside the car, Louise asked Jana if she was alright. 'You're looking pale and tired' said Louise.

'Yes, I'm fine, the flight was a little rough and seemed longer than it was, I'm just a little tired that's all' said Jana

'Well you just relax there; it won't be long before we are home' Louise said.

Jana did as she was told and quietly sat in the back of the car, watching the scenery go by, before nodding off to sleep. Jana woke to see that Joe was pulling into the services, it was raining they covered their heads and ran into the services. Finding a table to sit at, Louise asked Joe to order for her, she then excused herself and left Jana to sit alone at the table. Joe returned and finding her alone, he told Jana that he had to agree with Louise that she was looking pale. Jana just smiled, the smile, however, Joe noticed did not reach her eyes. He decided against saying anything else and thought he would speak to Louise later. A short while after they headed back to the car and it continued to rain for the remainder of the journey, the roads were getting waterlogged, and the motorway was very much like it was the evening that she had the accident.

Jana felt nauseous and held on tightly to the seat, hoping that Louise and Joe would not notice, she had not seen Joe watching her in the mirror, he had become aware of her anxious state and slowed the car down. With the change in speed, Jana unconsciously began to relax a little. Joe smiled to himself and hoped that she would enjoy the remainder of the journey. By the time they reached the house, the heavens had opened, and the rain was coming down even worse than before. Louise rushed Jana in through the front door while Joe got her bag.

'Come on let's get you a nice cup of tea and warm you up, you look ghastly' said Louise before taking her into the kitchen. Jana was grateful to Louise and Joe for fetching her from the airport and thanked them both with another hug.

They chatted for a while over the tea, Jana asked how Rachel was. 'Rachel has a nice baby bump now, and she is glowing,' Louise went onto tell Jana how they had been up to visit her and that they would be back the weekend after next to see Jana, this was the first time Louise had seen Jana smile since she picked her up from the airport. With a change of subject, Jana explained the situation with her home and how there was a need to get new tenant's, first there was a need to go and see how the house was looking and if there were any repairs required. Jana started to yawn, 'You really should rest Jana' Louise said and showed her the room she was staying in. Thanking her, Jana went to have a laydown. Darkness complete darkness, Jana could not see anything, then slowly streetlights began to glow an eerie glow, engine sounds and men shouting in the distance could be heard. A man began shouting out 'Run Jana run.' Scared Jana began to run, there was fog all around her as thick as pea soup, Jana could not see where she was running to, her legs were heavy, and it felt like she was running in thick mud, she began to scream.

The men stopped shouting; Jana could hear footsteps running behind her; they were gaining on her. She banged into something no someone, it was the faceless man he grabbed her arms again and began shouting 'Where is it, where is it?' Jana had no idea what he was talking about, and she tried to tell him, he wouldn't listen and started to drag her back to the sound of the car engine. The air was still thick, and she was unable to see where she was going. 'Let go of me, please let me go' Jana's pleas were ignored, and the man tightened his grip. The sound of footsteps running towards her echoed in the eerie light. Jana was pushed to the floor, the sound of men fighting, she forced her eyes to see what was happening through the darkness, Jana was too afraid to lift herself up off the floor, the fog appeared to be getting thicker, it was getting harder and harder to see what was happening around her.

Jana jumped as she was grabbed again, this time it was gentler than before 'Jana, are you alright, Jana, Jana answer me, please.'

'Brandon…' Jana called out

'Jana, open your eyes, it's me, Joe.'

Opening her eyes, Jana began to cry bitterly, the dreams were getting worse, more sinister and darker. Louise came into the bedroom with a glass of water for her. 'Jana, I have asked our doctor to come and see you. You cannot go on like this, your exhausted.' Louise said.

'No, no, I'm fine. Honestly, it was just a nightmare.'

'You have had these nightmares since the day I met you, I'm sorry Jana you need to be seen by a doctor, said Louise. Joe nodded in agreement. Jana did not have a chance to argue as the doorbell rang, Louise went to let the doctor in. Following his introducing himself to Jana he asked Louise and Joe to give them some privacy.

Louise did not look pleased to be told to leave but did as she was asked. 'now young lady, Louise tells me you have had these nightmares for some time, is that right?'

'Yes, that's right' Jana said, feeling it would be futile to try and lie to the doctor.

'How are you sleeping?' the doctor asked.

'Some nights are better than others' Jana said.

'Right, I am going to give you a prescription for some sleeping pills, I want you to ensure me that you will go to your own GP when you get home, he can then look up my notes of recommendations'

'I will doctor, thank you very much' Jana said, smiling.

'Don't be angry with Louise; she is just a good friend.' The doctor said as he let himself out of the room. Jana was not angry, but she was disappointed with Louise, she felt that Louise should have talked to her before calling the doctor out.

Louise looked sheepishly around the door. 'I'm sorry Jana, but you really scared me this time, we found you on the floor and Joe had to lift you back onto the bed.' Louise said.

'On the floor' said Jana

'Yes, you were cowering in the corner. Jana, please tell me what's going on I want to help you.' Louise said, pointing to where they had found her. Jana told her about the dream, how it had made her fear for her life and scared her witless. She said about the faceless man, his dragging her towards the car, the darkness and creepiness of the lights and the thick fog. 'It sounds like it came straight out of a horror movie, no wonder you were scared.' Louise said. Jana simply nodded. Louise held Jana while she let the tears flow until she could cry no more. *"The poor thing needs to let it all out,"* thought Louise.

'Right, let us get you refreshed, Joe has gone to get us a fish and chip supper.' Louise said. She showed Jana where the towels were kept, before leaving her to take a shower in the on-suite.

Jana relaxed a little, the water pouring over her aching body was soothing. After getting dressed, she went down into the kitchen where she found Louise making a pot of tea, she sat down and heard the front door opening, Joe was back with the food, Jana did not really feel hungry but thought it rude not to at least try and eat something. They chatted as they ate, Joe asked her where her cottage was and offered to take her down, 'We can see what's needed, and I can help with any renovations and repairs' Joe said.

'That's very kind of you, but you have your own work to do' Jana said.

'Nonsense, I'm my own boss. I have people working for me, and I need a change of scenery' Joe said, smiling. Jana did not have the energy to argue, smiling she thanked them both for their help. Supper was finished, they went into the living room to watch the television. The news was on, they watched as the story about the cruise liner going up in flames, filming from people's mobile phones showing the desperation of the rescue operation.

"No cost has been spared by the owners of the cruise line; the closest liners and other rescue teams had been sent to aid the rescue. The highly trained staff have removed the passengers in the lifeboats, those who were injured, frail or very young had been airlifted. The fire was at the opposite end of the ship. they

have been able to use the helipad to help with the rescue, and the owners have sent as many helicopters as they can to help."

The news presenter continued to speak and was about to hand over to his colleague in the Caribbean who was interviewing the owner of the cruise line. As he was about to introduce the owner, Jana's phone rang, and she left the room. 'Hello,' Jana said as she answered.

'Jana it's me, Charlotte.'

'Hello sweetheart is everything alright' Jana asked.

'Come back Jana I'm scared; daddy has not come back. Everyone is whispering around me, and no one will tell me where daddy is' Charlotte said as she began to cry. Jana tried to reassure her, but with her crying and with the discussion being over the phone, she was finding it difficult to reach out to her. 'Charlotte, listen to me ok, hang up the phone, and I will call you back on the house number, make sure your grandparents are there with you. I will call you in ten minutes' Jana said, hoping that she had got through to Charlotte.

Chapter Ten:
Home Once More

Jana rang Charlotte at the house as promised. Martha answered the telephone. 'I am so sorry Jana; Charlotte has become distressed since you and her father left the house' Martha said.

'I'm sorry too, I couldn't stay, not with the way things were' Jana said.

'I understand Jana, I do. I am worried about Charlotte, though. Brandon always calls her to say goodnight, he never last night, and now she is terrified that something has happened to him.' Martha explained about Brandon's work situation and how he had to deal with that, believing that this was the reason he had not called Charlotte. 'You must have seen it on the news, Jana. The cruise liner that caught fire.' Martha said.

'Yes, I've seen that and understand the difficulties that he must be under, but a little girl would not understand' Jana said.

'I have tried to explain things to her, but as I said, she is so afraid that he will not be coming back. Please see if you can talk to her' Martha asked with a worried tone in her voice.

Martha passed the phone to Charlotte and giving the child a chance to stop crying, Jana was able to talk to her a little better. 'Hello, little missy.' Jana said

'Hello Jana, when are you coming home?' Charlotte asked with sadness in her voice.

'I will come and see you as soon as I have dealt with things here.' Jana said with her fingers crossed she did not want to mislead the child but did not know what else to say.

'Charlotte, I know that you are a very clever little girl and that you understand that daddy has to work' Jana said

'I know, but he never said goodnight to me, he always says goodnight Jana you know that.' Charlotte said with a quiver in her voice Jana hoped that she would not start crying again.

'You need to give him a chance Charlotte; he is busy trying to help some people who were hurt. Your father is alright, I promise you, he is just busy, that's all. I bet he will call you tonight.' Jana said, trying to keep a cheerful tone to her voice.

'Really Jana do you think so. Thank you, Jana, I love you' Charlotte said before hanging up the phone.

It was Jana's turn to cry now; she missed the child so much; she could feel her heart-breaking. Louise asked Jana if everything was alright, Jana explained that Charlotte had become upset because her father had not said goodnight to her. Jana told her about the child telling her that she loved her, it was too much for her and Jana began crying again. 'It sounds to me that you love Charlotte as well' Louise said. Jana nodded, she explained that she had told Charlotte that her father was busy trying to help rescue the people on the cruise liner, get to safety and how she had promised her he would ring her tonight. 'I hope he does after me promising her, I would hate to think that my assumption he will call her might upset her further.' Jana said.

'There is nothing you can do about that tonight. I think you need to get some sleep you will be heading off early tomorrow.' Louise said. Jana hugged Louise and said goodnight, she shouted goodnight to Joe and went up to bed. Jana was not ready to sleep, she was worried about Charlotte and needed to know that the child would be alright.

Jana called on Celeste and asked if she would speak to Charlotte's angel asking them to remain with her until her father rang. Celeste reassured Jana that not only were Charlotte's angels with her but that her mother was also there comforting her. 'Now little one you have a task of your own to do tomorrow, you need to rest' Celeste said

'I can't rest, I keep having these nightmares' Jana said

'Yes, I know, little one. These are not simply dream's or nightmares, but they are messages, and you need to learn to understand them'. The angel said

'How, how am I to do that?' Jana said.

'You must first learn to remain calm in your dreams. It is only then that you will stand back and see them for what they really are.'

'I will try, but they are so dark and nasty' Jana said

'Look for the bright light and know that I am there with you. Now child time for you to rest' Celeste said shimmering as she left. Jana lay there for some time, she knew she was blessed to have an angel, Jana knew that she was especially blessed at seeing her angel. This was something that not everyone could do.

Jana felt her angels love around her for some time before she fell into a deep soothing sleep. As she dropped off to sleep, she prayed that she would not dream that night. Jana did not know how long her body or mind could last without a decent night's rest. Waking the following morning to the smell of bacon and fresh coffee, she felt refreshed. Once dressed, Jana headed down to the kitchen, finding Louise and Joe there. Louise spoke to Jana over her shoulder while cooking the breakfast, asking how she had slept. Jana reassured her that she had slept very well and that she was feeling a lot more rested. Louise was pleased with this, as was Joe. They had a long journey in front of them to the cottage. At some point during the night, Louise had decided that she would be going with them, *"it will be interesting to see where Jana had grown up"* Louise had thought. As they ate their breakfast, Joe discussed the route they would be taking and the length of time it would take them to get there, they made plans to have regular stops on the way.

The car was loaded, and they made their way, during the journey Jana's thoughts began to wander, she wondered what Brandon was doing and why he hadn't phoned Charlotte. Jana was secretly becoming concerned and prayed that he had not been injured during the rescue mission. She thought back to the time on the landing outside Charlotte's room. Her stomach made a little flip as she recalled how Brandon had grabbed her, she had thought that he was about to kiss her when he let her go. Jana watched him as he had descended the stairs hoping that he would look back and see her. He never did, he continued to walk away, it was at that moment that Jana had felt her heartbreak a little and promised herself that she would not allow him to do that to her again.

Jana's phone rang in her bag, she did not recognise the number, she answered the phone cautiously. 'hello, Jana is that you?' Jana recognised the voice instantly; it was Brandon.

'Hello Brandon, what can I do for you?'

'We need to talk Jana' said Brandon,

'What do we need to talk about? There is nothing to talk about Brandon' Jana said

'Please Jana, I need to explain what's happened' Brandon said.

'You do not owe me an explanation, Brandon; you owe your daughter an explanation. I suggest you go and talk to her about it' Jana said as she hung the phone up on him, believing that he was going to explain why he had not called Charlotte. Louise and Joe had listened to the one-way conversation, they did not dare to impose and ask what had happened, the tone in Jana's voice when she was speaking to Brandon had told them she was in no mood to talk about it. On the other end of the line, Brandon sat staring at the phone receiver, he could not believe that Jana had hung the phone up, on him. He knew she was angry with him but had not realised how much or why.

Brandon had returned to the house in the middle of the night and went straight to his study. He could not get Jana out of his mind, dealing with the cruise ship fire had merely distracted him for a short while. When Brandon was not busy working, all Brandon thought about was Jana and how right his father-in-law had been when calling him a fool. Brandon tried to call Jana back, he really needed to explain how he felt. This was something that that would have to be done in person, Brandon told himself when she would no longer answer his calls. He picked up the phone receiver and contacted Richard Wilson, he needed to know where Jana lived other than she was from the UK. Brandon needed to go and visit her himself, there was no other way that Jana would accept his apology. He had read all the background information that he had already paid Richard to get, he did not, however, have her home address, and this was vital to him.

Richard was about to refuse to get the information when he realised that there was a difference in Brandon Black, he noticed that his tone was a lot less aggressive. Brandon did not sound as nasty as he had in previous conversations. Richard promised to do his best in finding her for him. After speaking to Richard, he picked up the whiskey decanter and went to pour himself a glass, when he had second thoughts. Brandon placed the whiskey decanter down, thinking *"if I am going to win Jana over, I am going to have to change my ways, and this is one of them."* Instead, he sat by his desk and reread the information that Richard had dug up on Jana. Brandon had realised early on that Jana was a strong-willed woman, who had the strength to give to others even though she was having a difficult time herself. What he did not realise until now was just how robust Jana really was.

Jana was also thinking about Brandon, they were halfway through the journey when they stopped at the services. Jana went to order some coffee and cakes while Louise and Joe went to get freshened up. Joe walked back in, and Jana waved at him to come over to help carry the tray back to the table. Sitting down, they saw Louise coming back, she sat down and put her fingers through her hair asked, 'Is that better.' They both laughed as they recalled how Louise had fallen asleep in the car and how horrified she was that her hair was messy when she woke up. Jana excused herself, she did not feel up to chatting now and made the excuse she wanted to look in the shops. Jana's mind was elsewhere she picked up items and looked them over automatically, she had not taken in what she was looking at or if she really needed anything. All Jana wanted was a distraction from her thoughts, something that did not come easily.

Jana went back to the table; her mouth was dry; she needed a cold drink. She asked if the others wanted one before going to the counter. Joe asked for lemonade while Louise and Jana both had water. Walking back, she saw that a man was watching her, when she looked over the man looked away and covered his head. *"not again, I'm going to have to talk to that man sooner or later, he is not going to follow me around anymore."* Jana thought to herself. They all made their way back to the car; time was moving on, and they wanted to arrive before it got dark. Jana started napping in the back of the car, and when she woke, they were nearly at their destination. They arrived at the cottage and Jana went to her neighbours to get the key. She let Louise and Joe into the cottage, 'I'm just going to nip to the corner shop for some milk and things' Jana said.

Jana made her purchases and started to walk back to the cottage when she saw the man watching her again, she shouted at him to leave her alone, threatening to call the police. The man turned on his heels and ran. Jana had thought it was Richard before, she knew now that it wasn't him. Jana felt it better not to tell Louise and Joe as it would only worry them. Smiling, she walked into the cottage and put the bag on the kitchen counter, anyone for a cuppa she said light-heartedly, she didn't feel that way but didn't want them to worry. 'Oh yes please, and then you can give me a tour of this delightful cottage' said Louise. Jana showed her around the upstairs, 'There really is not much to see, it's just a three-bedroom cottage. It's nothing like your home' Jana said.

'Nonsense, it's beautiful' said Louise. They made up the beds, and Jana went to pull the curtains in her room when she saw the man again, leaning against the lamppost looking up at her. Jana drew the curtains quickly and hoped that he would go away, she was beginning to feel frightened again. *"who is this man? What does he want with me? and why is he hiding his face from me?"*

Jana's thoughts were racing through her head the questions coming one after the other at speed, she needed to pull herself together; she could feel the anxiety build up inside herself and knew she could not go down that road again. Jana showed Louise where her room was, 'No on-suite here I'm afraid' said Jana showing her where the bathroom is.

'Oh Jana, you have such a beautiful home' said Louise. Jana thanked her and promised to show her around the village in the morning. Joe had already been busy making a list of repairs by the time the ladies had gone back downstairs. He listed them for Jana and told her he would go to the shops in the morning for what was needed for the repairs. Jana gave Joe a big hug and thanked him for his help. They sat by the open log fire Joe had lit earlier, Louise made them all a hot chocolate.

They chatted about mundane everyday things until past midnight, before retiring to bed. Jana hugged them both and said goodnight before going up to her room. Jana could not resist looking out of the window, she was relieved to see that the man had gone. Lying in bed, she prayed for a good night's sleep, she still felt drained and put it down to not sleeping properly. Rest did not come easy, Jana kept thinking about Charlotte, she had been really upset the last time that Jana had spoken to her. It started to rain heavily outside, Jana listened to the sound of the rain hitting the window, she made a mental note to ring Charlotte in the morning. Jana fell asleep listening to the rain and began dreaming the same dream, the fog was as thick as ever only this time Jana could see through the mist. There seemed to be a glow around her, Jana realised that the light was her angel, she felt safe knowing that her angel was with her. Jana watched the dream as if watching a television program, scene by scene.

The men were there again, holding a gun to another man's head and forcing him into the car. He turned to face her; she could see it was Justin, the faceless man was also there, he turned to look at her and began running towards her, grabbing her he was demanding to know where the stuff was. Jana kept telling him that she did not understand what he was talking about, but he would not have it. The faceless man started to shake her violently, she was not afraid, and she did not feel the aggressiveness of the shaking. The light engulfed her, and the faceless man disappeared into the fog. Jana woke up remembering everything that she had seen, she felt calm as she ran through the images in her mind. What did the men want with Justin? Why were they threatening him? Is that why he disappeared? Many questions were going through her mind; they would have to wait to be answered. It was a relief to Jana to wake from the dream without screaming and shaking. Jana knew that she would soon work out what the nightmares meant, and she got herself dressed and went downstairs.

Louise and Joe were still in bed Jana tried to keep as quiet as possible, the house was small, and the noise travelled quickly around the little cottage. Jana kept herself busy making a list of the items in the kitchen that needed replacing, some of the tableware had chips in and there were very few knives and forks left. Jana decided that she would replace everything and changed the list to suit the needs of the kitchen. Louise joined her in the kitchen, 'How did you sleep Jana' Louise asked. Jana told her about the dream and what the angel had said, she told Louise how she could see her ex-boyfriend and how he was being taken at gunpoint. 'I just don't understand why' Jana said. Louise simply smiled; she did not say anything, Louise could never understand what Jana was going through. Louise remembered seeing George at the funeral parlour, and that was an experience, but what Jana must be going through Louise could not endeavour to even try to guess. Had she not seen George herself, she would think Jana to be having mental health problems.

Louise sent a silent request to Jana's angel, "if you really exist, then please help Jana find peace of mind, help her to find her role in life."

Louise was getting worried about Jana the way she had returned so suddenly, Louise did not believe it was because of the cottage, Jana could have had an agent to deal with that. Louise watched Jana for a while as she pottered around the kitchen, before going to give Joe a call. He would need to get up soon if they were to go shopping. Jana decided to go for a walk she needed to clear her mind, she told Louise her plans and putting her coat on against the cold and the rain of the October morning she headed out of the door. Jana was used to walking in the pouring down rain, she sometimes made her better decisions then. She needed to decide what she was going to do with the rest of her life, there was no need for money her parents and grandparents had seen to that. Jana was exceptionally well off; she had been brought up; however, to respect money and not to abuse it.

The decision she had to make now was whether to remain at the cottage or to move to the city. Jana knew she would have to find a job to occupy her mind so that she did not return to the realm of despair. Jana remembered clearly how that had felt following the accident, what kind of job she would look for she would need to think about, as she did not feel confident enough to go back to her old job as a physiotherapist. Jana walked down through the village toward the beach and had not been here for some years, Jana never forgot how this beach had made her feel, especially when walking on the beach and the feeling there her grandparents were there with her. She was a child when she came to live in the village after the death of her parents and had no choice but to move in with her grandparents. Jana loved them dearly, and they did all they could to bring her up the way her parents would have. Her mother and father had adored her,

Jana's grandparents made sure that she knew this and told her every day of their love for her.

Jana was so caught up in her own thoughts that she did not notice the man following behind her. Jana reached the beach and strolled across the sand, her grandfather had told her it was always better to come to the beach to look for sea glass after the winds and rains had been. He told her how the sea would wash different colours of sea glass up onto the beach. Jana found a piece of yellow glass in the shape of a wing. As she held it in her hand, she thought of Charlotte and the necklace that she had the jewellers make for her from a piece of sea glass. She continued to walk along the beach occasionally stopping to look out to sea, it certainly was a different view, she missed the warmth of Lanzarote and the azure colour of the sea, here the sea was murky and dark looking, especially in the later months of the year and it could be quite depressing to look at.

Making her way back to the cottage, Jana turned to walk back up the beach, as she turned around, she noticed someone looking in her direction from the top of the cliff, she could not make out what they looked like or who the person was. Shrugging she continued to walk back, looking over occasionally at the clifftop to see if the person was still there. Getting to the road, Jana looked one last time, whoever they were they had gone. Jana had an uneasy feeling about it, she reached the gate just as the postman was leaving, Joe had already picked the mail up off the floor. There was some mail for her previous tenant, she placed them in another envelope and addressed them to her son as arranged. There was also a letter from Collette, an old friend that Jana had grown up with going through school and university together. They had laughed together, cried together, played together and double-dated together. Both girls were very fond of each other and had become like sisters over the years. Fate, however, had other ideas for them.

The letter appeared to be a long one, Jana made a pot of tea and sat to read the letter from her friend in the kitchen.

"Hi, Jana,

I am so sorry that I have not been in touch for a while, things have been hectic this end. Jana, I have a special question to ask you. I am sorry it is going to have to be in a letter, I pray it reaches you at the cottage. I have tried to call you to ask in person but have had no success in getting you to answer the phone as apparently, you have moved out of you flat in the city. Jana, Shane has asked me to marry him. Please, please say you will be my maid of honour. I am on edge waiting for you to answer me so please let me know as soon as you have this letter. I have put my home and mobile numbers on the back of the letter, just in case you have forgotten or lost them."

All my love

Collette XXX

Jana's friend had moved to London for work, and this is where she met Shane. Jana had not seen her for some years, and although they did not live in each other's pockets, they did keep in touch. Of course, she would be her maid of honour, Jana picked up her phone and dialled the house number on the back of the letter, there was no answer, so she tried her mobile number, again there was no answer. Jana left a text message to let her know that it would be an honour to be part of her wedding. Jana asked Collette to call her when she had the chance to read the message so that she could get up to speed with the plans and what Collette expected from her exactly. She finished her call, and Joe asked if she was ready to go shopping, 'there really is not much that you need to fix on the cottage' Joe said.

At the shops, Joe went off to find what he needed, and Jana and Louise went to the kitchen store to buy new things for the Kitchen. She chose an orange coloured tableware and picked up some new cutlery. She also purchased a new matching toaster and kettle as well as some new saucepans. When they finished, they met Joe in the shop's café? They made plans for Jana to show Louise the village while Joe got on with the jobs that were needed to get the cottage back to its glory. It had started raining heavily outside, Joe left the ladies by the front door of the shop and went to get the car, by the time he reached the car he was soaked through, he helped to pack the car, and they made their way back to the cottage. On the way back Jana started to get the uncomfortable feeling and knew that someone had passed to the other side, as they turned the corner, they could see a fire engine, police car and ambulance. The police were redirecting them as the road had been closed.

The journey took them along the coastal root, and despite the rain, there were some beautiful views. Jana started thinking about the glorious views in Lanzarote again and wished she was back there, why she did not really know she just felt the need to be there. Her thoughts reminded her that she needed to call Charlotte. A half-hour later they were back at the cottage, Louise put the kettle on while Jana and Joe unpacked the goods they had bought. Jana removed all the old stuff and placed it in the garden shed ready to be disposed of, after this, she went upstairs to make the call to Charlotte.

The phone rang out for a little time before Charles answered the phone. Charles sounded really pleased to hear from Jana, she asked if she could talk to Charlotte, he asked her to hold the line while he went to get her. Before Charlotte could come on the phone, Brandon had picked it up. 'Jana, please don't hang up; it's me, Brandon.'

'What do you want Brandon, I've only called to speak to Charlotte' Said Jana

'We really do need to talk Jana; I owe you an apology, and I would like to give you that apology in person' Brandon said.

'There really is no need to apologise, Brandon, now if that is all, please put Charlotte on the phone' Jana said. Brandon did as he was asked, he did not want to alienate Jana he needed to get her on his side.

'Hello, Jana' said Charlotte.

'Hello, little missy, are you alright.'

'Yes, I'm good, I'm glad you phoned, when are you coming back Jana, when?'

'As soon as I can, sweetheart' Jana said through gritted teeth. They spoke for some time before Jana had to say goodbye. Brandon had tried to get the phone off Charlotte before Jana had the chance to hang up, he was not successful and felt disappointed.

Jana lay on the bed, she, missed Charlotte so much, the tears started to run down her cheeks. She knew that it was not just Charlotte; she was missing, but could Brandon be trusted again, and what connection did he have with the private investigator, and why was he giving Brandon information about her. Needing to know Jana pulled out the phone number for Richard Wilson from her bag and called him. 'Hello, Richard Wilson, private investigator How can I help?' Jana was about to speak when his voice continued and asked for a message to be left, she had no option but to try again. Jana went into the bathroom to freshen up as she did not want her friends to see her crying. Downstairs Louise was making some sandwiches and tea, Louise shouted up to Jana that they were ready 'On my way' said Jana coming down the stairs. Jana told them about her chat to Charlotte and how she again asked Jana to go back to Lanzarote.

Jana and Louise discussed her reasons to go back and why she should not go back. Joe had sat there quietly listening when he broke the silence saying' I think you need to look deep into your heart Jana. no pun intended.' They all started to laugh, deep down, Jana knew he was right. 'Now where shall we eat tonight' said Joe

'We could eat locally; they do some lovely bar meals down at The Flying Dragon. It's in walking distance as well' Jana said

'Sounds good to me' said Louise.

'Then it is a date ladies' Joe said as he blew them both a kiss from across the room.

'He can be so silly sometimes' Louise said. Jana could see that the love between husband and wife was solid and wished for that herself one day.

Joe pottered around while he waited for the ladies to get themselves presentable, he had decided to wear a T-shirt and jeans. He never did understand why women had to dress up to the nine's even to go for a drink locally, and the length of time it would take them to get ready always baffled him. His wife would simply say that he was a man and would never understand and with that point, all he could do was agree. With their coats on and ready to fight the chill, he held out his arms to them and asked, 'Are you, ready ladies?' Louise and Jana looked at each other and hooked their arms through Joe's 'a double date; this is going to be an expensive night for me' said joe laughing. Within a couple of minutes, they were at The Flying Dragon. Joe took their coats and hung them up on the coat hangers provided, the ladies found a table while he went to the bar. He returned with a couple of red wines for them and a pint of stout for himself. He also brought back the bar menu for them to look at a little later.

They chatted for a while, and Louise remembered that Rachel was coming to see them next weekend. 'They can come here, there is plenty of room. That is if you two are going to stay awhile' said Jana. They agreed that they would stay, Joe stating the obvious that it would take 'Oh at least another week or two' before the work on the cottage was complete. With it decided Louise said she would ring Rachel in the morning and let her know that she would be coming to see Jana at her cottage, remembering Rachel's nosy streak she knew she would love to see more of Jana's life. Jana told them about her friend Collette, and the plans to marry her fiancé. She said to them that she had been asked to be the maid of honour and how happy she was to have been invited. 'Ah, so that answers your earlier question of whether to stay in the UK or go back to Lanzarote. At least for a short while anyway' Joe said. Jana nodded in agreement, it did seem the decision had been made for her, *"maybe fate has a hand in the decision"* she thought.

They had not realised when they came into the pub that there was going to be entertainment, the barman told Joe that they had a male vocal singer starting at nine o'clock. They all agreed that it would be nice to stay out for a while but thought better of waiting for the food as it would spoil the entertainment. They looked at the menu, Joe chose steak, and Jana and Louise both chose scampi. It was not long before the food arrived and with a full bottle of white to go with it. 'Oh, you are spoiling us, Joe' Louise said, smiling at her husband. Joe nodded and smiled back at his loving wife. Jana watched on feeling a little green with envy, in her heart of hearts she wished them well. Jana finished her food quickly, she had not realised how hungry she was, thinking back it was not surprising she had only picked at her food over recent weeks. They chatted while they ate, it was not long before the wine had been finished, Joe went to the bar to get them another bottle and another stout for himself.

The artist was all set up and ready to sing, there had been sheets of paper and pens placed on the tables for those who wanted to request a song. He started with the song I Believe. Jana must have been a bit worse for wear than she had first thought as she began to sing along to the words, the artist came over with his mic and complimenting her on her voice sang along with her. Jana usually would have shied away from such a thing, but tonight she could not stop herself from singing out the words. When the song finished the whole of the bar applauded her along with the artist, 'Now ladies and gentlemen, that is what I call a warmup' he said as he held out his hands to applaud her again. Louise sat there with her jaw open, 'You are a dark horse Jana, who knew you could sing like that' Louise said, smiling. Jana just smiled for some reason she was feeling good, and she just wanted to share those feelings with people around her. What Jana had not seen was the stranger who she had seen watching her since she had returned home.

The man had been sitting at the corner of the bar, just out of view from Jana he had placed himself in a position where he could see her, but she would find it difficult to see him with everyone around the bar. He had been watching her for some time, it was not her that he wanted, but was waiting to see if Justin would show up, his bosses had instructed him to watch Jana in the hope that he would show his face because she was back home. He had not been in luck so far and had spent some nights watching her cottage while another one had been instructed to watch Jana by day. He was getting annoyed that he had to hang around, if the guy they were after did not show up soon there would be a need to go and ask her himself, that he promised himself would be something that she would not like very much.

He continued to watch her in the pub then followed them back to the cottage. He stood on the corner by the lamp post for some time, until he saw that all the lights were off, he then went and sat in his car hoping that this would be the night that Justin showed up. Jana settled into bed, unaware that a stranger was watching her home, she felt a little more relaxed with Louise and Joe around. Jana had enjoyed her night out and had not had herself a night out like that in a while. Even though she was feeling relaxed she still had difficulty falling off to sleep as thoughts of Charlotte floated through her mind, Jana wondered what the little girl and her father were doing.

Chapter Eleven:
Follow Your Heart

Brandon had been unable to get Jana out of his mind when he worked, she was a distraction always in his thoughts and in his dreams she was there. When he played with his daughter, Jana was there, *"why the hell is this woman plaguing my life"* he thought. Charles and Martha had also seen a change in Brandon, he was not as angry all the time. Well… he was still annoyed with Jana, and they knew who he was blaming for that. Charlotte had also moaned at her father, she wanted Jana back, she missed her a great deal, they all did. The adults had sat in the lounge talking one night when the subject of Jana came up. 'You know son, you really should not have let that young lady leave said, Charles.

'What could I do to stop her Charles, you know the situation I was in that night' Brandon said.

'Yes, yes I do you had a tough night' Charles said.

Martha could not keep a civil tongue, 'Well that didn't stop you from asking one of us to ask her to stay?' Martha said as she screeched out the words at Brandon.

'Martha, nothing any of us could have said would have kept her here, she was determined to go' Brandon said.

'Have you tried to speak to her since she left here? said Martha.

'Yes, Martha I have, on more than one occasion, now do you mind if we change the subject please' Brandon said with a sigh. He was missing Jana more than anyone would ever know. They all sat in silence for a while each one not knowing what to say next. Martha and Charles wanted to continue the conversation about Jana, they wanted their son-in-law to see how foolish he really was. Martha could not hold her tongue for long. 'Brandon you really need to let my daughters spirit rest, it is time you moved on. You need to get a new mother for Charlotte, it is what Lucy would have wanted. We all know that.'

Brandon gave her the most disgusting look, but he knew; he knew she was right. Brandon loved Lucy to the bones, and he knew she would not want their daughter to grow up without a woman, a mother by her side. Brandon said nothing and rising from the chair left the room to go to his study. Charles looked at Martha, 'Why did you say that to him?' he said. Martha shrugged her shoulders and walked over to the windows. Charles understood and joined her, holding her in his arms. They both loved their daughter dearly and knew that Martha was right in what she had said to Brandon. Brandon was angry with them both, he was more annoyed with himself, he went into his study to contact Richard Wilson, to remind him that he wanted Jana's details, including her address and the addresses of her friends. Brandon wanted, no… he needed to see Jana again.

Brandon spoke to Richard for around half an hour. He told him that he needed to return to America for some time and that he wanted the information as soon as possible. Richard assured him that there would be closure soon and that Brandon would have all the information within a week. After arranging to call Richard when he was back in the states, Brandon went back into the lounge, he needed to have a serious talk with his in-laws. When Brandon walked in and found them staring out of the window and seeing they were upset went to pour them all a drink. He asked them to join him, once they were all sitting, Brandon explained why he had been acting the way he had.

Brandon told them that he felt he was deceiving his wife and that being with another woman he thought might upset them and his daughter. 'Oh Brandon, we love and miss Lucy very, very much. Had it been that dreadful woman you took to the work Christmas party last year. Well... I think we would have both been very angry' Martha said.

'Quite right, but Jana. No son, Jana is right for you, for both you and Charlotte' said, Charles.

'Yes, and I believe that Jana would not even try to take the place of Lucy. She would be a perfect mother to Charlotte in her own right' Martha said.

'Yes, and we also know that she would keep Lucy's memory alive for Charlotte, and all of us would help with that too' said Charles.

Brandon looked at his in-laws, they had been the replacement parents that he needed since his parents passing. Brandon knew that he did not deserve them and that he had been horrid to them since his parents and wife had gone. Brandon told them that of his plans to go to America and to take Charlotte back with him. Brandon explained how he needed to get her the help that she really needs. Brandon asked if they would join them, he told them that he would need their support now more than ever. 'We will always be there to help you, Brandon, but what is this all about' said Martha.

'Jana believes that Charlotte has feelings in her legs and that she stopped using her legs as a way of punishing herself for her mother and grandparents' deaths. Jana agrees with you Martha that Charlotte is blaming herself for the crash because she was playing up in the car' said Brandon.

'How does Jana know this' Charles said.

'Jana is a qualified physiotherapist, something I should have realised and didn't I'm afraid. Jana recalled reading about this kind of thing before.'

'What is it?' Martha said.

'Jana thinks it is something called "Conversion Disorder" she believes that Charlotte has transferred her stresses after the accident to a physical nature instead' said Brandon.

Brandon went on to tell them that he owes Jana an apology. How Jana had left a letter on his desk. The letter explained what Jana believes Charlotte needs to help with her health problems. The main thing Charlotte needs is to see a psychologist, Jana also advised an exercise program and gave me the names and numbers of people she knows personally who could and would treat Charlotte in the right way. Brandon told them how he had doubted her. 'That is until I had the report from Richard,' Brandon said.

'You set a private detective on her' Charles said disgustingly

'Oh Brandon, no wonder the woman is so angry with you' said Martha.

'I know Martha, I know, and I promise you I am going to make things up to her, but Charlotte comes first, and if Jana is right then I need to get her home to find her the best psychologist that New York has' said Brandon. Both Martha and Charles nodded in agreement.

Brandon told them that he planned to leave for the states, as soon as possible. He thanked them for their support and went to arrange the flight back to the states. Before arranging the journey, Brandon went up to speak to Charlotte, she had been in her room resting. Sitting beside her bed, Brandon told her what Jana had said and the plans to go back to the states for her to get the best help he could. Brandon asked his daughter how she felt about going to see a psychologist. He told her that the psychologist would be talking to her a lot to help her think through her problems and how to help solve them. Charlotte looked at her father her brows coming down over her eyes in a puzzled look. 'Daddy why would you pay someone to do that when I could just talk to Jana' Charlotte said innocently. Brandon put his arms around his daughter and hugged her so hard she had to tell him to stop because she could not breathe. Martha walked into the room just as he was kissing her on top of her head, Charlotte laughed and told her grandmother that her father was silly. Martha smiled and asked if she was ready to join them for some food, she asked Charlotte what she would like to eat. Charlotte looked at them and laughed as they said Pizza at the same time. Brandon promised to order in the pizza after he sorted the flights to the states. 'Make sure I can watch movies daddy' Charlotte said.

'Anything for you, Charlie' said Brandon as he left the room.

The flight was arranged to take them two days later, he ordered the pizza as promised, and while he waited for the pizza, he tried to contact Jana to thank her for the advice and to tell her they were leaving for New York to get the help needed. Jana heard the phone ring, she picked it up and saw that it was his number, she was not in the mood to talk to Brandon and refused to answer it. Louise had been watching her, she was getting concerned that Jana was beginning to shut herself off from them and knew that it would affect her terribly if she lost contact with Charlotte. They had spoken to Rachel, and it was decided that both Rachel and Stuart would be arriving early. Rachel was impatient and could not wait to see them again. Jana busied herself, getting the room ready for them. Louise and Joe went to the supermarket to pick up more groceries. While they were shopping, Louise expressed her concerns about Jana. Joe agreed with her but advised against interfering. 'Jana is a strong-willed woman she won't thank you for it' Joe said. Martha looked over at him, he knew that look, he knew Louise would not be able to resist.

The bedroom was finished and ready for Rachel and Stuart. Jana looked out of the windows and saw that the sun was shining, she decided to go for a walk around the village the quaint little shops selling their goods were interesting, and she had not been down to them for some time. As she walked along, Jana began to feel uneasy it was not the same as before she could feel eyes on her, she looked around but could not see anyone. Jana shrugged it off as paranoia and forced herself to continue with her window shopping. After going into some of the shops and picking up a few things, she went to a quaint little café for a cream tea. Jana sat facing the window and chatted to a few of the locals who knew her. While talking, she saw the same man pass by the window and in doing so looked directly at her. She tried to ignore him and continued to chat, her phone began to ring, it was Louise letting her know they were on the way back. Jana knew they would be passing the café and asked if they would pick her up on the way back.

Jana ordered some cream cakes to take home with her and waited for Joe's car to pull up outside, she quickly got in the car and looking around for the man saw him standing on the corner. Jana did not say anything to the others but had become very uncomfortable with the situation, she could feel her heart beating against her chest, *"if I see him again, I am going to call the police" she thought to herself.* They arrived back at the house to see Rachel knocking the door, hugging her Jana asked what they were doing there, reminding her that they were not expecting her for a few days. 'I am so sorry to impose on you like this Jana, but I couldn't keep her still she was so excited to be seeing you she practically begged me to bring her and I didn't want her stressing' Stuart said as he pointed to her pregnancy bump.

'It's ok Stuart, I understand and your more than welcome to stay as long as you want' Jana said hugging him. They all went inside the house, Jana looked over her shoulder, trying not to show the others. Jana caught something moving in Stuart's car out of the corner of her eye.

Stuart noticed that she had seen the dog and went onto explain 'It's our little dog Misty, I am hoping to find a kennel locally while we are here.'

'Don't you dare, the dog is as welcome as you are, we had better check that the others don't have allergies first though' Jana said laughing. She went inside and spoke to Louise and Joe; they were more than happy for the dog to stay. Misty soon made herself at home and curled up in front of the fire going to sleep almost immediately. Louise made some tea as Jana went to get the cakes *"I'll have to cut the cakes in half and share them"* Jana thought. Jana had thought she had purchased three cakes when she opened the bag; however, there were two boxes with a selection of five cakes between them. Jana did not recall asking for the five cream cakes, Jana only remembered asking for three. She gave a silent thank you to the angels for the cakes and placed them all on a serving dish and put it in the centre of the table along with some tea plates for them to choose their own from the selection.

Jana had always been partial to a cream cake, eating one always brought back fond memories of when she and her grandfather would sit down and share a big cream puff cake. She remembered how he would put his finger in the cream and touch the tip of her nose with it, Jana would always try and lick it off with her tongue. They would laugh and laugh till they cried with laughter. 'Earth to Jana,' Rachel said. Jana apologised for drifting off into the past and told them what she had been thinking about. 'It's good to have memories' said Louise and they all nodded in agreement; their mouths too full of cake to speak. The women cleaned up the dishes while Joe helped Stuart to bring in their things from the car. Jana showed them where their room was, she told them she was expecting a full update on what the doctors were saying about the pregnancy and how it was progressing. Rachel hugged her and said that she needed a lay down first. Jana and Stuart left her to it and went back downstairs.

Joe had pulled out a board game and asked if they would like to join them, they had been playing the game for over two hours when Rachel came down asking what the time was, as she was getting hungry. Louise said it was six o'clock, and asked what Rachel would like to eat. Rachel told them that she had been craving a Chinese meal for a couple of days. 'Chinese it is then' Jana said finding a menu in the drawer and she placed the order over the phone. The men took Misty for a walk, while they waited for their meal to arrive, Jana and Louise got the table ready, and Rachel made them all a tea. Jana heard her phone ping and checking found an email from Gloria had arrived, she had remained friends with her and kept in touch via email and phone. Jana also noticed there were a few missed calls from Brandon's house number.

Brandon had tried to contact her numerous times, to let her know that they were leaving. He was disappointed and hurt that she would not answer his calls.

Brandon could not think about Jana now he had to push her to the back of his mind, he had given her a chance to answer him or call him back, It was time his daughter to come first, Brandon packed the bags into the car, and they all left for the airport where Brandon has chartered a plane. They boarded the plane for a direct flight to New York. Brandon had arranged for a car to pick them all up at the airport in New York. Once settled in their seats, buckled in and the captain was sure that they were all safe, the plane took off. Charlotte put her headphones on and watched films, while the adults talked about the plans for Charlotte before they started to nod off to sleep.

Brandon looked over to Charlotte and seeing she was sleeping changed her seating into a sleeping position, Martha and Charles did the same. Brandon watched as they all fell asleep one by one. He pulled out his laptop and replied to the work emails he had received, there were 150 emails in total. One by one, Brandon answered them, then beginning to yawn himself, he repositioned his seat slightly and had soon joined the others in having some sleep. The journey had gone so smoothly that none of them had even noticed it go by until the captain was waking them and asking them to put their seats in the upright position and buckle up. The plane landed safely, they disembarked and headed through to security and the arrivals lounge and out to the waiting car. They were soon home and unpacked, Charlotte was in familiar surroundings, and she let everybody know she was as well. She was ringing her friends and letting them know she was back. She rang her uncle and asked when he was coming home.

Charlotte had so many questions for so many people, but the final question was for her father. 'When is Jana coming home?' Martha distracted her and took her to get something to eat. Charles asked Brandon if he was alright, he had seen the pain in his face after his daughter had asked him the question. Brandon reassured him that he was and excused himself so that he could arrange for the psychologist to see Charlotte. The arrangements were made for the psychologist to attend the house, Brandon rang Richard to see if there was any progress on finding Jana. Richard had all the information that he needed and said he would email them straight over. Brandon opened the email to find out the addresses, and then made solid plans to go and see Jana, surely, she would not ignore him standing right in front of her. Brandon called Martha and Charles together and told him of his plans to go and speak to Jana.

Brandon told them of the arrangements with the psychologist and the physiotherapists that Jana had recommended. Assuring them that he would not be leaving for at least a week as he had some work to do at the New York office and that he wanted to be here for Charlottes first meeting with the people who were going to get her better. Brandon made them promise that he would not tell Charlotte that he was going to see Jana as he did not want her to get disappointed if she did not come back with him.

They both reluctantly agreed, they knew he was only trying to protect Charlotte; still, they did not like lying to their granddaughter. Brandon made the arrangement to travel to Britain, he had been there many times on business so Charlotte would not be any the wiser if he told her he was going there for work purposes again. Back in Britain, Jana was enjoying her time with her guests, they reminisced about Lanzarote and spoke about the good times and the bad. 'Why don't we go down to the pub, we can enjoy a pint and a chat there' said Joe. Stuart agreed, there really was not much choice for the ladies it was either join them or stay in, they chose to join the men.

Walking along with the others, Jana felt a little left out as she watched each couple linking arms and walking together. She did not show them, but Jana had been feeling lonely of late, not alone of the company she had plenty of that, but lonely without a man to love and to love her back. Only she was in love with a man, and he was across the water. They arrived at the pub, there were quite a few people in there, and they were lucky to find a table big enough for them all. The men went to the bar, Joe brought a bottle of red wine and a glass of orange juice for Rachel, he told them that there was a comedian in the pub a little later, 'Apparently, he is hilarious, and that is why it is so full tonight.' Joe said.

The men sat by the bar for a while chatting, while the ladies got the update of the baby. 'How is the baby doing' Jana said

'The doctor is really pleased; the weight and length are right, and there are no signs of any physical health problems with the baby' Rachel said, smiling.

'That is good news' Louise said hugging Rachel.

'Do you know what you're having, and have you thought of any names yet?' Jana said.

'No, we decided against knowing the sex of the baby, we want it to be a surprise. Yes, we have thought of some names but have not really decided on them yet' Rachel said. The men joined them as the artist was about to begin. They listened and roared with laughter at the comedian, they could see why there were so many people in the pub. He was a funny man., a short while after the comedian started Jana began to have a headache. She told them that she was going to head back to the house, she needed to lay down. 'I'll walk you back' Joe said. 'No. No you stay I will be fine; I just need to rest' Jana said.

Jana had already given each couple a key so that they could come back and forth as they pleased. She hugged each one and left the pub to walk back to the house, shortly after Jana had the feeling that she was being watched again, Jana looked around, but could not see anyone else about. She shrugged off this feeling and put it down to being wary of her surroundings in the dark. Jana arrived at the house and could hear Misty barking inside. Jana opened the door and walked in, turning on the lights, she could see that the house had been trashed, every room had been searched through. Frightened, she grabbed a long umbrella from the stand, by the front door, what she was going to do with it she did not know. Jana saw that the back door was open, it had been forced open, it was time to call the police. While she waited for the police, Jana placed a chair behind the back door to keep it closed.

Jana called Louise and explained what had happened, they all came back to find Jana sitting in front of the fire with Misty curled up on her lap, the police arrived at the same time. The police took statements from everyone, making lists of what was missing. Joe asked if there had been a lot of break-ins in the area and was informed that this was the first in many years. The police asked if they had seen anyone hanging around, Jana told them about the man she had seen on more than one occasion. She could not give a description other than of slim build wearing dark clothes, and that he wore his hood up. The police reassured Jana that they would do everything they could to find the culprits who had done this and left their cards with names and numbers before leaving. Joe had already set to fix the back door making a note in his mind to put extra locks on both doors. Stuart helped Jana and Louise to tidy up, Rachel made them all a hot drink. It was evident that Jana was upset, and they all needed to be there even more for her now. Jana had not been feeling safe for some time and did not really understand why but felt that she was in a lot of danger. Jana wished that Brandon was with her now, someone who could hold her through the dark lonely night ahead of her.

Brandon was waiting at the airport in New York, he had made the first meetings with the psychologists and physiotherapists with Charlotte, she was happy to work with them. Only because it was what Jana wanted, she had told her father quite firmly. Sitting in the first-class departure lounge with a whiskey in his hand, his thoughts went to Jana and the gentle way she had handled his daughter's tantrums, quite nasty outbursts on times. He had first-hand experience of them, but Jana had coped with them so well, that he was seeing Charlotte have less and less of them. Brandon knew that he loved Jana, he had for some time and hoped that it was not too late and that he would be lucky enough to be able to get her to accept his apology. The announcement was made for them to board the plane, first-class passengers were called first. Brandon was shown to his seat and offered a drink as soon as he sat down. He knew it would be a while before the plane took off as there were so many people left for boarding the aeroplane.

While the plane remained on the ground, he opened his laptop and answered all the emails sent to him. Brandon did not want anything to disrupt his plans. He had already booked a hire car and a hotel to stay in, it was about half-hour from Jana's home address. The seat belt sign lit up, and the announcement came from the captain to let them know that they were preparing for take-off. Brandon put his laptop away and placed his seat in the upright position, he watched as the other passengers did the same, and the staff collected the glasses before going to find their own seats. Brandon had chosen a night flight; this would give him the chance to have some rest before arriving in Britain. The plane was soon in the air and levelling out. He brought out his laptop again, he needed to keep himself busy, Brandon was feeling impatient he needed the plane to be in the UK right now. This was not going to happen, and so he buried himself in his work to distract from all thoughts of Jana.

Brandon had been working for some time when the air steward who was allocated to his area of the plane came across to confirm that his meal would be ready soon and asked if he would like to make his way to the shared lounge. Once there he was brought over a drink's menu, Brandon ordered a single malt and water. The meal and drink arrived shortly after, Brandon ate his food slowly, his mind drifting back to the times when he watched Jana play with Charlotte. *"yes, Charles and Martha are right. I should never have let her go; I should have fought for her sooner"* Brandon thought. His meal finished, he went back to his seat, he found it had been made up into a bed. He freshened up before laying down, the steward brought him a hot drink over, and it was not long before he was sleeping. Jana, however, was not as fortunate, she was exhausted.

Jana had not slept at all throughout the night, she worried that whoever had broken in would come back, she was worried about Rachel and the baby. They had all tried to reassure her that everything would be alright, but the uncomfortable feeling she had been getting was becoming more and more intense. Jana had called on her angel for help, there had been no reply, she felt as if she had been abandoned by the angels and questioned why they would not answer her. Jana did not realise that the angels could not intervene with what was meant to be. She tried to remain in her room and not get up too early for fear of disturbing everyone else, by half-past four in the morning she had had enough. Jana went downstairs and made some tea and lighting the fire sat with Misty as the flames took hold. 'I will have to get myself a little dog' Jana said to Misty as she resided herself to a lonely life free from men, free from the one man she truly loved.

Brandon was told that it would not be long before the plane landed, he got himself up and went to get a shower before breakfast was served. He had slept well and felt good, he just had to be a little more patient. Brandon had arranged to go to the London office before heading off to the hotel, it would take him nearly three hours to get there, he was used to British roads and the traffic and knew that there would be a delay. Brandon took his time eating his meal and drinking his coffee before taking up a chair in the lounge to read the papers that were provided. Brandon had promised to call Charlotte and looking at his watch thought better of doing it straight away and would give it another half hour before doing so. The plane would be landing in about an hour, so he needed to make sure he did call her in time. Brandon set the timer on his phone to remind him. If there was one thing he had noticed, it was that his mind was so full of thoughts of Jana, he forgot everything else.

The captain reported that the weather was terrible for the landing in London, 'there are heavy showers of rain and crosswinds' he said. His alarm went off, and Brandon called Charlotte as promised. Brandon asked Charlotte to promise him that she would do as she was told and that she would do all the exercises as well. 'I will, daddy, don't forget my present will you' Charlotte said before saying goodbye to her father. The announcement came that they were getting ready for landing, Brandon buckled up and waited, he was not fond of the arrivals. Brandon remembered being on a plane that was practically landing sideways. It was not a good feeling and one that was never forgotten. The landing was smoother than he had expected, yes there had been some crosswinds, and the rain was indeed torrential, but the pilot managed to land the plane without a hitch.

Brandon made his way through international arrivals and security checks before picking up his bags. He walked out into the arrivals lounge and saw a familiar face holding up his name. 'Thank you, John' said Brandon as he took the hire car keys from him. Brandon had used this company for many years and knew most of the staff working there. John told him where the car was parked, knowing all too well that John would have to make his way back to the city, Brandon offered him a lift which he accepted gracefully. Travelling through the centre, John told him that the business was having difficulties and that there was a possibility that it may be going into liquidation. John thanked Brandon for his custom and said that it may be the last time they ever see each other. As he dropped him off Brandon wished him well, he knew that the company was a global one, he had not however heard on the grapevine that it was in trouble.

Arriving at the London office, Brandon met up with the managers and solicitors employed there. He directed the solicitors to find out if there was any truth in the liquidation of the transport company and told them to let him know immediately. Then Brendon set down to sort out the problems that the London team were having. Brandon was there so long that he had to remain in London for the night, he was determined to sort things out before he left in the morning. He was still at the office at one-thirty in the morning before things were finally resolved. A hotel room had been booked earlier, meals ordered and ate in the board room, now it was time for rest. Brandon went to the hotel room where he undressed and lay on the bed, exhausted he remained until nine o'clock in the morning. Getting up, he showered and readied himself for the journey ahead of him. He made sure he had some breakfast as the route was going to be a long one; the weather was terrible, and the driving conditions were atrocious.

Brandon set off at ten thirty, it took him over an hour before he reached the motorway, putting the radio on he made his way down the busy and wet road to his destination and the woman he loved.

At the cottage, Jana had made breakfast for them all, she could see the concern in their eyes and promised to have a soak in the bath and to try and get some sleep. Louise had heard her sobbing through the night, she was getting very concerned about Jana, they all were. Jana filled the bath and lay in it, soaking in the heat of the water. She was in there for an hour or more when there was knock on the door, it was Rachel seeing if she was alright. 'Yes, I'm alright, Rachel, thank you' said Jana.

'I've put a cup of tea on your bedside cabinet, please try and get some sleep' Rachel said. Jana promised that she would, she got out of the bath and put on some pyjamas before going to her room, she could hear them all chatting away downstairs. Jana was grateful to have friends like them, but she missed being part of a family. Getting into bed, she drank her tea, before slipping off into a deep sleep.

Downstairs they were all talking about Jana, each one of them having the same concerns and conclusions as to what was bothering her. 'She has been like this since returning from Lanzarote' Louise said.

'Something must have happened to her there' said Rachel

'no, I think she misses that little girl so much' Louise said. None of them had realised that Jana had fallen deeply in love with Charlotte's father. Jana never told any of them how she felt for fear they may say she was foolish as she had not known him for very long. It was some time before Jana woke, she looked outside, and it was beginning to get dark. Joe and Stuart had taken Misty down to the beach for a walk leaving the ladies to talk to Jana. Placing a cup of tea and a sandwich in front of Jana Louise told her about how worried they all were about her. She explained how they believed it to be because she was missing Charlotte.

Jana did not want to deal with it all now and let them believe that it was because she was missing the child. Jana took the tea and sandwich into the lounge and sat in front of the fire, talking to them about Charlotte. The door opened, and Misty came in, shaking her wet fur all over them, they all began to laugh, and the conversation was forgotten. They decided to have a film night and once Misty was cleaned up, they sat in front of the television. They were halfway through the film when there was a knock on the door, Jana went to answer it and gasped in shock as Justin stood in front of her.

Jana could feel the anger mount up in her chest' what the hell do you want' Jana said, she could not forgive him for leaving her the way he did.

'Don't be like that babe' Justin said as if nothing had happened.

'Don't be like what, Justin. I haven't seen you in over two years, don't be like what' Jana repeated.

'I know, I know. I can explain' Justin said. Jana had only just noticed that he was repeatedly looking over his shoulder.

'What have you done, Justin?' said, Jana.

'Can I come in, Jana please' Justin said.

'No, I have visitors, I don't ever want to see you again' said Jana. Justin looked her up and down, realised that she was in her dressing gown and took this to be that she had found someone new. Justin knew he was defeated and pulled her close to hug her as he did, he kissed her on the lips before leaving. Across the street stood a man, frozen to the spot, he had also taken in the fact that she was wearing bedclothes.

Brandon had been watching them, he had not been able to wait to see her and made it the first thing he wanted to do when arriving at the village. He had not expected to see what he saw and broken-hearted left in the darkness of the night. Getting into his car, he vowed never to fall in love again. Jana had not seen Brandon as she watched Justin walk up the street, there was a screech of tyres, and she watched as, in front of her, the dream she had been having was coming to life. A black car pulled up, and two men got out, they did not grab Justin as in the dream, they just stood there and shot him before getting in the car and speeding off. Jana ran over to Justin, kneeling she held his head in her lap. 'I am so sorry, Jana, I am so sorry I deceived you, I promised to marry you and love you for the rest of your life. I am sorry he repeated as his life slipped away from him.

The others had all run to Jana's side, the police and ambulance were on their way. They were too late; he was gone, Justin was gone, and Jana was in shock. Louise and Rachel took her back inside while the men waited for the emergency services. Jana told them about Justin and who he was to her, and how she had not been able to find it in her heart to forgive him. She wished she had now.

It was several weeks later, and her four friends had returned to their own lives, Justin's shooting was history. She had been questioned repeatedly by the police, and they told Jana that Justin had been involved in drug running and that he had kept some of the drug money and drugs, selling them on for himself. They had not found any leads as to why he had been shot but believed it to be the men he stole the drugs from. The police had reassured her that any further information they found would be given to her. Jana kept thinking back to the night that Justin was shot, yes, she grieved for him, but her feelings of loss were stronger for Brandon. He had returned to New York he felt nothing but anger believing that Jana had always had a lover back in Britain. He told Martha and Charles what had happened how he had seen her in her nightclothes kissing a man and hugging him goodbye. Brandon felt betrayed by Jana and would never fall in love again. He told them that he would allow Charlotte to remain in contact with Jana via the phone. Brandon, though hoped that he would never see Jana again.

Looking out of the frost-covered window at the snow laying on the ground, the tears spilt down Jana's face. The tears were for Brandon and the unrequited love that she felt for him. Sitting in front of the fire with a glass of wine in her hand, she stared into the flames and thought back to Lanzarote again, she thought about Charlotte, and her heart was breaking as she thought about Charlotte's father. As the tears rolled down her cheeks and her heart missed a beat, Jana asked her angel if she would ever see Brandon again? Turning, Jana saw the all too familiar light and watched as her angel appeared and said to her 'You already know the answer to the question my child, you decided that before you ever came here, your heart has the answer… follow your heart.' Jana turn back to look int the flames of the fire and wondered if she would ever see Charlotte and Brandon again…

The End